David Christie Murray

Hearts

Vol. I

David Christie Murray

Hearts
Vol. I

ISBN/EAN: 9783337048396

Printed in Europe, USA, Canada, Australia, Japan

Cover: Foto ©Andreas Hilbeck / pixelio.de

More available books at **www.hansebooks.com**

HEARTS

I.

HEARTS

A NOVEL

BY

DAVID CHRISTIE MURRAY

AUTHOR OF
'JOSEPH'S COAT' 'A LIFE'S ATONEMENT' ETC.

IN THREE VOLUMES

VOL. I.

London

CHATTO & WINDUS, PICCADILLY

1883

LONDON : PRINTED BY
SPOTTISWOODE AND CO., NEW-STREET SQUARE
AND PARLIAMENT STREET

PREFACE.

A FOX who had lost his tail set forth before his fellows the advantages he had accidentally discovered, and advised that the fox family should go tailless. It is not recorded that he made converts.

An American writer of fiction has offered to his fellow craftsmen and the world his opinion that 'all the stories have been told.' If this gentleman cannot invent a story, it is probable enough that the mental attitude he chooses to take is something of a comfort to him. But his compeers are not likely to accept the method he offers.

In one way the statement that 'all the stories have been told' is a feeble truism. In another it is a silly falsehood. It is just as obviously true on the one hand, and just as obviously foolish on the other, at this hour, as it was before the foundation-stone of English literature was laid.

English fiction, even in this day of small things, scarcely needs to be defended against the complacent insolences of this writer, whose literary example will only be followed by those who are confronted with a Hobson's choice. We are rather at a barren epoch now, and readers are compelled to endure a good deal of commonplace. Our one great living writer is old and seems inclined to rest upon his laurels, but there are new men coming who will bring new powers, and will even, in the teeth of our American friend, invent new stories. There are some of us already at work who are quite resolved that when we can no longer create a story we will cease to write.

After that bright day which saw Thackeray and Dickens and Eliot and Reade and Lytton all shining together, we endure a natural night of comparative dulness. Yet the reading public may forgive an English writer of fiction (whose claims are small but who loves his craft with all his heart) if he refuses to accept without protest the critical conclusions which affirm that the craft is dead. Those conclusions have been discussed with absurd gravity by people who ought to have known better than to accept them seriously. If a new departure in fiction is to be made at all, let it lead us to the sovereign passions which are immortal in man,

and not to the frivolous speculations in science
and theology and human nature which are only
the mental fashion of an hour.   Paint the age
by all means, and paint it truly, but do not
appraise yourself as an artist whilst you can
give us nothing but photographs.   And if you
are to be a fictionist at all, make up your mind
at once that invention is a faculty essential to
the pursuit of this most difficult of the arts.

D. C. M.

HEARTS.

CHAPTER I.

A YOUNG man attired in the height of the fashion of 1870 was no very strange figure in the Strand on any evening of that year ; and Tom Carroll, though splendidly bedizened, excited no unusual admiration or regard. A handsome young Briton, with a gay, honest face and friendly eyes—at first sight a likeable lad—he was pleasant enough to look at, as he walked, head well up and eyes smiling, prosperous and contented with the world, and evidently disposed to be on kindly terms with all men. It was in the dusk of a summer

evening, and the spire of St. Clements' Danes
was backed by a celestial golden fleece, which
no Londoner regarded.　Corners and by-places
were beginning to be filled with shadows; and
the street gas-lamps and the lights in the shop-
windows had a sort of twilight brightness.　At
such times you may walk about in a shabby
suit of clothes, if you will; and Tom Carroll,
running full against Antonio Baretti, an old
acquaintance of his, beheld at first no change
in him.

This Antonio Baretti was an Italian and an
artist, and only a little while ago he had begun
to be a person of some note.　Even if he chose
to go shabby, that might be one of the affec-
tations of successful genius.　But Baretti was
not yet so eminently successful that he could
afford to cut a man like Tom Carroll, whose
social position was indisputable, whose pockets
were full of money, and whose life was spent
in the pursuit of all the arts at once, and in

companionship with wealthy and titled people, who relied upon his judgment in the matter of plays, pictures, and music. For Tom was a dilettante of the most agreeable and popular type, and a *persona grata* in all manner of high places. It was more than a little odd, therefore, that Baretti should make an evident effort to avoid him ; and it was all the more singular because the two youngsters had been rather enthusiastic than otherwise over each other's achievements. They were good fellows, both, into the bargain.

'Why, Baretti,' said Tom, stretching forth a hand and laying hold of him by the lappet of the coat, 'won't you speak to a fellow ?'

'I—I beg your pardon,' said the little Italian ; 'I was in a hurry and did not——' His voice trailed away, and he left the sentence unfinished.

'You're not well,' said the young Englishman, reaching out a second hand and laying it

on the other shoulder. The artist, with an
outward gesture of both hands, seemed at once
to deprecate inquiry and to indicate his own
condition. The velvet coat was threadbare and
crumpled. The little man's linen was un-
pleasantly yellow and much disarranged. His
face was pallid, and his chin and cheeks were
stubbly. 'You're not well, Baretti. What's the
matter?'

'I am not well of late,' said the shabby
artist; 'but how are you? And how are all the
little people—the opera, and the sonata, and the
gavotte? And how is the landscape? Well?'

'Come and dine somewhere,' returned Tom.
The other repeated that outward gesture of the
hands. 'Come and dine. I want to have a
talk with you. Where have you been hiding
yourself?'

'I have not been in hiding,' said Baretti,
with an undeceptive pretence of gaiety. Tom
Carroll, with a hand on each of the little

man's shoulders, looked him up and down. A button was missing from the shabby velvet jacket, and the loose threads from which it had escaped hung down untidily. The patent eather boots were cracked and broken.

'Tell me the truth,' said Tom, rocking him lightly to and fro. 'Come home with me to my chambers, and tell me the truth about yourself.'

Baretti blushed fiercely, and then turned white. His lips began to tremble, and when he stole a look at his companion there was a gleam of tears in his black Italian eyes.

'I will go with you,' he said huskily, 'and I will tell you everything.'

'Very well,' said Tom, feigning a somewhat rollicking tone. 'Come along.'

He took Baretti's arm and they walked westward together, not saying much by the way. The Italian was thankful for the gathering darkness, being conscious that his companion's splendour made his own dismal aspect far more noticeable than before. The young Englishman was in his glory, for here was genius out at elbows and altogether down upon its luck, and he the happy deliverer of it, and the man appointed by Fate to set it on its feet again and establish its goings. There was no better-hearted youngster in London than Tom Carroll; and if he exulted a little at the chance of doing such a service, he was none the less sorry for the other's misfortunes, whatever they might turn out to be. His heart warmed over Baretti as they walked along together, and he felt more friendly to him than he had ever done before. To be five-and-twenty, and to have a good heart, and a full purse, and a friend in need of you—is there a better way to happiness?

When the pair came to No. 20, Montague Gardens, Tom Carroll admitted himself by a latch-key, and led the way upstairs into a comfortably furnished apartment, where shaded lamps and handsome curtains gave things a well-to-do and homelike look.

'Sit down, Baretti,' said Tom, pushing the other gently by the shoulders. Baretti's lips were trembling more and more, and his eyes were so dim that he dared not raise them to Tom's face. 'So bad as that, old chap?' said the youngster gently.

Suddenly, to Carroll's terror and amazement, the little man wrenched himself free, and throwing himself upon his knees beside an arm-chair, burst into hysteric tears and sobs. The Englishman stood awkwardly in the middle of the room, not knowing what to do or say in such a case, and, therefore—being wise without knowing it—doing and saying nothing. In a while Baretti composed himself, and, still kneeling there, began to wipe his eyes with a woful handkerchief. The host recovered himself a little also, and bustled about noisily in the next room, lighting candles on the mantel-shelf and dressing-table.

'Here, I say, Baretti,' he called, when the sobs had all ceased, ' you'll want a wash before dinner. I'm going down to order dinner now, and if you want anything, I've put out a lot of things on the bed.'

Then he withdrew by another door, and whistled ostentatiously on the landing to show that he was outside. This young man was a Briton, though an artist, and tears would have seemed a shame to him in almost any circumstances. When Baretti had first broken out crying, Tom would have been glad for the floor to open, and he suffered acutely from a reflex shame. Half an hour had gone by before he returned to the room, and then Baretti was standing before the fireplace, not altogether at his ease, but clean and clean-shaven, and in white linen, and looking vastly improved all over. In these altered circum-

stances he was a handsome little man. His
eyes were full of feeling and intelligence, and
as beautifully soft and bright as a dog's; his
coal-black hair tumbled picturesquely about
his head in handsome, disorderly profusion;
his hands were white and shapely; his figure
was well set, and his face well-featured and
attractive.

'Dinner's coming up in a minute, Baretti,'
said Tom, for the mere sake of saying something.

'Carroll,' said the artist, stretching out both
hands to him.

'What is it?' asked Tom, taking them in
his own. 'You're in trouble of some sort.
Tell me what it is. If I can help you, I'll do
it. Now, what is it?'

A tap at the door announced the advent of
the maid, and the young Englishman dropped
his friend's hands in some embarrassment.

'You shall tell me after dinner,' he said,

when the girl had retired; 'she will be interrupting us every minute until then.

The Italian assenting, the two sat down in
silence. Dinner was served, and the guest
attacked his soup like a man who meant
business; but he pushed the fish away scarce
tasted, and recoiled from the tempting cutlet
which followed.

'No appetite?' said Tom.

'Too much,' returned Baretti, with a poor
attempt at a laugh. Tom nodded gravely,
with a sympathetic glance at his guest, and
on the girl's next appearance bade her clear
away.

'Now, what is it?' asked the Englishman,
when they were secure against further interruption. The manner of the question was
engaging, and expressive of a hearty wish to
be of service. 'What is it? Tell me as
much as you can, and let us see what we can
do. What is it?'

'I am broken,' said Baretti, with a tremulous lip—'absolutely and completely broken—without a roof—without a shilling—a lost man!'

'Without a roof?' the other asked, in amazed pity.

'I have lain upon the benches in St. James's Park these four nights,' the little Italian answered. 'I have eaten nothing until now for four days.'

Tom, with a great show of righteous wrath, began to walk up and down the room, and to upbraid his companion, using much strong language, with a view to the disguise of his own emotion, after the British fashion.

'You thundering little idiot! Hang it all, Baretti! Not to tell me! You knew where I lived all the time. I take it unkindly of you —I take it infernally ill of you, Baretti!'

'I was broken,' urged the little artist in extenuation. 'I did not know what to do.'

'Then, by George, sir,' cried Tom, 'you ought to have known! Here have I been going about just as jollily as ever, and I feel like a criminal now I know about it. You know very well, Baretti,' with a mightily injured look, 'that I have more money than I know what to do with. You know very well that you had only to ask me to have whatever you stood in need of. And, by gad! instead of coming up like a friend, and giving me the pleasure of helping you, you slink off and starve in St. James's Park. I tell you what it is, Baretti, I think it was unfriendly— confoundedly unfriendly!'

'I beg your pardon,' said Baretti, in quaint contrition.

'Tell me all about it,' Tom returned, being in a condition to trust himself by this time. 'That is—tell me what you can; and what I can I'll do.'

'I would have come to you rather than to

anybody,' said the little Italian, with out-reaching hands and moist eyes; 'but I was broken at heart, and I did not care—no; not for anything.'

'Tell me,' said Tom.

'Did you know the Count Carambola?' asked Baretti, turning upon his host with sudden passion.

'That hook-nosed, green-skinned ruffian, with the black moustache and the bald head?' demanded Tom. 'I knew him as well as I wanted to.'

'We thought him honourable and wealthy,' cried Baretti, beginning his story with a fiery gesture of disdain.

'I didn't,' interjected Carroll, drily. 'What about him?'

'I will tell you what about him,' said the artist, declaiming with such gesture as only an Italian uses. 'The Count is a villain, a hound, a cur—a personage sunk in the depths of infamy! He came to me three months ago, when my picture was but newly hung at Burlington House, and he asked that I would lend him four hundred pounds. I laughed. I told him that when I had four hundred shillings I looked at myself as at a Rothschild. He also laughed. It was but an affair of a week, of a day, two days, three days; but he was unknown here to the English bankers. Would I back a bill for him? He knew so well no other countryman in London. Would I so far assist him? Then when his funds came would I sell him my beautiful picture at the Academy? Would I paint more beautiful pictures for his Villa della Luna? Will you credit me, I was so much a fool that I believed him? *Gran Dio*, Carroll! I believed him! Whom the gods would destroy they first make mad; and I believed him. But when we came to the money-lender, he did not care for my name. He would have a bill of sale.

That was the name. Do you know it? No. A bill of sale upon the poor little things in my studio, and a claim upon my picture at Burlington House. I agreed to everything gladly. The Count had the money, and in a week I missed him. Then comes one friend and another. "My dear Baretti," they say, "is it true that you have helped the Count? He is gone; he is flown; he owes everybody money; he does always so; he is an adventurer professed." '

'I could have told you that much at the first and only sight of his ugly face I ever had,' said Tom.

'Under a blow so crushing,' resumed Baretti, 'what do I do? I sit still in my studio, deserted of my fancies. I try to paint. I have forgotten that a black and a white make gray. I am helpless. By-and-by—about a month ago—the money-lender's people come, and sell everything, My picture sells at the

Academy, and they take the money for it. There is over and above a little handful of shillings, and that they give me. That goes, and I am a lost man.'

He ended with quivering lips, moved anew by the narration of his own wrongs and sufferings, and dropped dejectedly into an arm-chair that stood near.

'And, of course,' said Tom, 'you've never heard of the Count again ?'

The little artist sat like a statue of despondency, with his arms hanging helplessly at his side; but at this query he sprang to his feet, and answered with wild gesticulation :—

'The Count? He is flown to his own Phlegethon !'

'Best place for him,' said Tom, quietly. 'Let him stop there.'

'Willingly,' answered Baretti, with a bitter laugh, and dropped back into the arm-chair.

'Cheer up, old fellow,' said Carroll, patting

him on the shoulder. 'It's all over now. There's a stunning north light to the room overhead, and it will make a capital studio. I know it isn't engaged, and I'll just run downstairs and take it now. The bedroom at the back is thoroughly comfortable, and the place will suit you to a hair. We'll lay in whatever you want to-morrow ; and you'll soon find out again that black and white are not the only things to make a gray. You don't mind staying alone for five minutes? Cigars and wine,' pushing a box and a decanter forward on the table. 'Make yourself comfortable. Back in five minutes.'

There was a glow in Tom's heart as he ran downstairs to chaffer with the landlady about a set of rooms for Baretti. He approved of himself, and felt that he was a good sort of fellow. By-and-by he returned beaming.

'I've taken the rooms, Baretti. Come and have a look at them.'

The artist arose and followed him upstairs, moving like a man in a dream. Tom chattered gaily, pointing out the loftiness of the windows, and showing how the light could be arranged by moving the shutters, which had been cut across, by order of some former occupant, an artist. Next he marched Baretti into the bedroom, and dwelt at length upon its advantages, talking rather at random, lest the Italian should thank him.

'And now,' he said, on regaining his own rooms, 'you'll want money for your purchases to-morrow. It will be better not to run into debt to begin with. Suppose I give you a cheque at once?' He sat down to write it out, still chattering the while. A ring was heard, and shortly afterwards a tap sounded on the room-door. 'Come in,' cried Tom, slipping his cheque-book into a drawer.

'Mr. Mark, sir,' said the maid, opening the

door, and she retiring, the personage announced as Mr. Mark entered. He was not unlike the regular occupant of the room at first sight, but a second glance showed so many differences that it began to be surprising that any likeness had appeared between them. The most marked of these differences was in expression. Tom's face was full of light and gaiety. He looked frankly at all men, with a not unpleasing confidence in their approval of him, and pretty generally with a full approval in his own eyes. He was but a youngster yet, and was unaffectedly fond of people. He liked almost everybody; and that cheerful mood of mind was written on his good-looking countenance in letters of brightness. His visitor, though a handsomer man than Tom, had his personal beauties strongly discounted by an unprepossessing look of suspicion and dislike. It was likely, you might have thought, that he had but a poor opinion of men and women at large—possibly a poor opinion of himself in some directions.

'How are you?' cried Tom, heartily, rising to meet him. 'I didn't know you were in town. This is my friend Baretti, Mark. I dare say you remember his picture at the Academy this year. This is my cousin Mark, Baretti—Mark Carroll.'

Cousin Mark's glance took in the broken boots, the frayed shabbiness of the velvet coat —every sign of poverty the artist's dilapidated dress displayed. He bowed stiffly, and Baretti answered with a sense of discomfort and shame-facedness.

'I wouldn't have come to-night,' said Mark, 'had I known you were engaged. Shall you be in at twelve to-morrow?'

'Yes,' said Tom. 'Anything particular?'

'Rather particular,' answered Mark.

'Baretti will excuse us,' said Tom, brightly. 'Come into the bedroom.'

The little artist bowed frigidly as the new-comer passed him. Mark disregarded the salute.

'I'm in something of a hole, Tom,' he said, closing the bedroom door behind him. 'I want fifty pounds. Can you let me have it?'

'When do you want it?' Tom inquired.

'To-morrow, at twelve.'

'To-morrow!' Tom echoed, with a rather dismal face. 'I'm a little——' He cleared in a second. 'Come at three instead of twelve, and I'll have it ready for you.'

'All right,' said Cousin Mark, rather un-graciously. 'I'll be here. I say, who's that fellow?' He nodded backwards towards the sitting-room.

'You've heard of Baretti,' said Tom. 'Rising artist. One of the most promising young painters in London.'

'One would guess as much to look at him,' said Mark, with a smile. His smile was less agreeable than his habitual expression, and when that is the case, it generally augurs ill of a man.

'Oh,' said Tom, deceptively, 'that sort of man is often careless about appearances.'

'I suppose,' said Mark, 'he's on my errand. Came to borrow money, didn't he?'

'I asked him here to dinner,' Tom answered. 'He's a capital fellow—one of the best fellows in the world.'

'Everybody is " one of the best fellows in the world " with you,' said Mark, smiling again. 'I am one of the best fellows in the world myself.'

'Why, so you are,' Tom answered, laughing; 'I am another. Come in and have a talk with Baretti. You'll find him a charming fellow, I assure you.'

'No,' said Mark; 'I won't stay to-night. At three to-morrow. Good-night!'

The two young men came back into the

sitting-room, and shook hands. Baretti's head had dropped forward as he sat in the big arm-chair near the fire, and his regular breathing betrayed the fact that he had fallen asleep. Tom laid a hand upon his shoulder to awake him, and the artist, sleepily opening his eyes, stared at him for a second or two without recognition, and, rising, took two or three steps forward, before he was fairly awake.

' I beg your pardon,' he stammered ; 'I am over-fatigued.'

Mark nodded with his own smile, and gently pulled Tom from the room.

' Has that rising artist,' he whispered behind his hand, as they paused upon the landing—' has that rising artist ever obeyed the policeman's " Move on, there ? " He looked rather like it.'

' Pooh ! ' said Tom, in a disconcerted way. ' Three o'clock to-morrow. Good-night, Mark ! '

' I am ashamed to have fallen asleep,' said

Baretti, when his host re-entered the room;
' but I am very tired.'

' Of course you are,' said Tom, reopening
the drawer in which he had placed the cheque.
' That,' he went on, pushing the paper into
Baretti's hand, ' will set you going again, and
leave you a little margin.'

The broken artist looked from the cheque
to Tom, and from Tom to the cheque, like one
amazed; and before the Englishman knew it
the Italian was at his feet, clasping both his
hands, and pouring out an incoherent torrent
of thanksgiving.

' Nonsense, man ! ' cried Tom, half angrily.
' Get up, and don't make a fool of yourself.
You would have done as much for me if the
cases had been reversed.'

' No,' cried the painter, springing to his
feet and confronting his benefactor with outstretched hands and flashing eyes, ' I would not
have done so much for you. But now——

Am I a fiend to say that I should like to see
you in misery, in want, in disgrace, in despair,
that I might die to comfort you?'

'Bosh!' said the young Briton, with an air
of shame. 'I'm not going to fall into disgrace
and misery to oblige anybody. If you do want
to oblige me, Baretti, you can do it easily.'

'How?' cried the little man, with a fiery
gesture of interrogation, as if he would have
rent his friend to pieces. 'Tell me.'

'Forget the Count, and set to work again.'

'I shall find my chance,' said Baretti, with
an aspect of almost tragic gloom. 'You will
want me some day. I shall not die until I
have repaid you.'

'Why, man alive,' said Carroll, with feigned
impatience, 'you've only to set to work to be
able to pay me in a month!'

'To pay you what?' demanded the little
man. 'The handful of money that you lend
me? Yes. But the hope you gave me when

I despaired? The faith I had lost in human nature? The life I should have thrown away to-night?'

'You never meant that, Baretti?' Tom demanded, gravely. The painter's eyes fell, and his head drooped.

'Yes,' he said, stonily; 'I meant it. And but for you,' he cried, with new fire in his eyes and his voice, 'I should have done it. Carroll, I am yours—your friend, your brother, your servant, your slave!'

'All right, old man,' said Carroll, shaking hands with him. 'Say no more about it.'

'Good,' said Baretti. 'I will say no more. But it is true, and I mean it.'

It was good acting if he did not mean it. His eyes gleamed like black fire, and his lips quivered. When the two had parted, Tom reflected on the events of the night, and said to himself, not without satisfaction :—

'I ought to have made a friend.'

CHAPTER II.

THERE is a school of philosophers according to whose tenets it is easy to be philosophical. The aspirant to wisdom learns that there is little to be done but to set the basest construction on all human motives, and to believe and prophesy the worst in regard to all human actions. This royal road to philosophy has been pursued by notable people, and the man who travels by it is sure of certain obvious advantages. The clock that stands still tells the truth twice a-day, and the mental attitude which never varies will find itself justified upon occasion. It is an axiom with the acrid school that if you do a man a service he will hate you; and, like many other axioms of many other schools, it is true in some cases and false in others.

A man who takes another out of the streets of London and shelters him ; who takes him out of despair and brings him home to hope again ; who takes him from the dread of an ignominious finish to life and gives him new chances of fame and fortune, does what few men have a chance to do, and may fairly be said to have deserved gratitude. Tom had done an undoubted good turn to Baretti, but he had not looked for so volcanic a thanksgiving as the little man offered in return. Gratitude was not a sentiment but a passion with this hot little Italian. His benefactor filled his thoughts as a dearly-beloved mistress might have done. He deified him as young men in love deify their sweethearts. Tom Carroll was the noblest, the most generous, the handsomest, and the ablest man in the world to Antonio Baretti. For weeks after the artist's recovery from despair there were minutes when he laid down his brushes because he could not see his canvas for the moisture in his eyes, as he thought of the magnificent tender goodness of this best of friends and patrons.

My Lord Bellamy—a neighbour of Thomas Carroll the elder, in the country—had given Baretti a commission (of course through Tom's intercession), and Baretti was at work on a canvas measuring six feet by four, painting with prodigious ardour to the sound of Tom's violin, which came soaring from the room below. Thin cascades of scales, sonorous cascades of scales, sometimes a tune which made Baretti long to dance, and sometimes a plaintive air which made the emotional little fellow long to cry—these sounds arose almost continually, for some six or seven hours a day.

'Be witness for me,' the youngster would sometimes say to Baretti, quoting Mrs. Browning:—

‘ Be witness for me—with no amateur's
Irreverent haste and busy idleness
I wrought for art.’

And then, being newly inspired, he would go
back to his fiddling and saw sparks of light
and laughter, or long sweet sighs of musical
anguish, from the fiddle-strings.

You may believe that these were happy
days for the rehabilitated artist. Such hal-
cyon visions of fame as ardent young painters
have were with him often, and were always
sweetened by his gratitude, and his resolve to
show it and prove it to the world at large.
He had promises within him of such a brotherhood in art as the world had never seen.
Carroll could afford to work and wait for pure
art's sake, and would be hailed some day as a
great composer, and the king of fiddlers, and
Baretti himself was going to vault straightway
into fame by the painting of this one picture.
And when they were both great men, and the

painter was in the very ripeness and zenith of his day, he would go down to Tom's country mansion and enrich its walls, as mortal walls were never enriched before, with colour and sweet form. And they would be friends for ever, with no possibility of a wrinkle on the face of the young cherub of friendship who smiled so dearly now. A good little fellow, with a fine exaggerative heart and temperament, chokeful of gratitude, and love, and hope, and an ambition nine-tenths unselfish!

Master Tom, though not quite the paragon his southern *protégé* believed him, was worthier of this unstinted admiration than often happens, and being himself of a generous, open nature, and having done the Italian so brotherly a turn, he was of course immensely fond of him and interested in his successes. So these two lads of five-and-twenty loved and admired each other loyally—the Englishman with a shy sentiment and a purposely roughened outside to it, and the Italian with a downright openness of declaration which embarrassed while it pleased. The artistic enthusiasm of the one spurred that of the other, and they slaved away with ardour at their respective pursuits. Tom saw much less of the fashionable world in these days than he had been used to see, and, with the constant labour to which he gave himself, made real progress in his difficult art.

Cousin Mark was a frequent visitor at Tom's chambers, where he smoked Tom's havannahs and drank Tom's claret, whilst he listened with his own cynical grin to Baretti's encomiums on Tom and Tom's encomiums on Baretti. The painter was not merely rescued from seediness of apparel, but being provided with the where-withal by his moneyed friend, had blossomed into outrageous sartorial gaieties which somehow seemed to suit him. Tom had lent him in all a hundred and fifty pounds, and since Baretti was to receive three hundred for his picture, he

bore the weight of his money debt with
patience. He wore a velvet sacque to paint in,
and was generally to be seen indoors in a
gorgeous smoking-cap, and slippers in the hues
of sunrise dyed. Certain valuable meerschaum
pipes, which had been confided to the care of
mine uncle (to whose door the artist had found
the mournful road a month before), were in his
own possession again, and one of these always
gave a fitting finish.to the picture he presented.

Cousin Mark was not burdened with more
money than he knew what to do with. His
uncle—Thomas Carroll the elder—was not
disposed to be over and above liberal, and
Mark's profession of barrister was so far
unremunerative to him. Cousin Tom, on the
contrary, had plenty of money, having inherited
a few loose thousands from his mother, and
being in receipt of a comfortable additional
allowance from his father. Tom's position
from Mark's point of view was enviable.

There are two or three sorts of envy, only one of the kinds being criminal. But—not to beat about the bush—Cousin Mark's envy of Tom Carroll had a little of the criminal tinge in it. Mark had carefully trained himself into the belief that human goodness was a sham. and that nothing was done by anybody without an eye to the *quid pro quo*. Uncle Thomas gave him an allowance. Good. He flattered uncle Thomas, and believed himself expected to do so. Cousin Tom was ridiculously generous. Well, money was cheap with cousin Tom, and to that absurd order of mind it was worth money to be called a good fellow, and to surround oneself with sycophants. Mark begged from the father and borrowed from the son, and was properly sycophantic, with an undercurrent of cynical humour in his service, and an affectation of manly bluntness which more than redeemed him in his own eyes.

Now, Mark had a mania for getting at the

bottom of things, and from the first hour when he had seen his cousin and Baretti together their connection had puzzled him a little. Calling one evening he found Baretti alone and, quite unnecessarily, began to pump him.

'It's rather odd, Signor Baretti,' said Mark, 'that you and I should never have met until a fortnight ago, since Tom and you are such friends.'

'Ah!' said the Italian, with a bright and tender smile. 'We are old acquaintances, but the friendship is a new one. The friendship began the night you first met me here.'

And, eager to exalt his idol, the painter began to tell the story. He reiterated with profuse Italian action the history of the Count's wickedness, and he pourtrayed his own misery and despair. He acted the part of Tom Carroll in the Strand, the compassionate, the generous, the good; he enacted his own part at that memorable interview also, sparing in his description no breach in his boots or tinge of yellow on his frayed shirt-collar. He brought his hero and himself into the very room in which he told the moving story. He cast himself anew upon his knees and buried his head in the arm-chair in illustration of his own abandonment to sorrow. He sprang to his feet and spoke out of his chest in imitation of the admirable rescuer's cheery manner. There were tears in his lambent soft eyes as he lauded his preserver and swore fidelity to him.

London is pretty thickly provided with human contrasts, but it would not have been easy to find two young fellows wider apart in thought and feeling in all London's limits than the man who told and the man who heard this story. Mark listened with interest, and was even not without admiration. He admitted that—in the Italian style of art—Baretti's was a very fine performance. He thought that he had never seen the cynic's definition of gratitude so well illustrated. To say that he doubted the genuineness of Baretti's protestations would be to do Mark an injustice. He was certain in his own mind that the little man was a liar and a pretender—like other people. Only, he lied and pretended better than the ruck, being an artist and having command over what were called the emotions.

To Baretti such an injustice as Mark did him would have seemed impossible, even if he could have been brought to understand the mental condition which created it. Not to have been grateful would have been prodigious, and all his southern soul was given to his preserver.

'Where the carcass is,' said Mark to himself, 'there will the vultures be gathered together. If there were plenty for both I suppose no two would waste time in pecking at each other. But this Italian vulture is a big-beaked fellow—a fellow with an appetite. A hundred and fifty is a good-sized first mouthful ; and a mere flap of the wings won't scare that harpy. I must dig him in the ribs and pretty keenly. The British bird was only just in time, a fortnight ago, to secure a morsel one-third the size of the foreign bird's mouthful.'

Whilst he entertained these reflections Mark was pleasantly conscious of his own cynical humour and his own cynical candour. Curious how, if you show any man his face in the glass, he is not displeased with it. Execrable singers chant for their own amusement, and like their own voices. It is conceivable that the skunk esteems his own odour highly, and would have a poor opinion of eau-de-Cologne. And, quite as a matter of course, cousin Mark thought his own mental attitude admirable. If he had the penetration to see through Baretti's humbug, he had also the honesty to admit the truth about himself. And it would not be true of him to say that he began to hate the little painter.

Active sentiments of any kind did not come to him easily, and life, though a warfare, was to be gone through with no more passion than was necessary. There are men who would skewer you if you could not otherwise be got out of their way, and if it were safe to do it, without mercy, and without rage—just at the bidding of a cold hunger for your share of things—and Mark Carroll was of them.

It is one of the vulgarest errors in the world that men are unhappy in proportion to the narrowness of their sympathies. The garotter's conscience is the cat-o'-nine-tails.

When Mark came to look at it fairly and squarely, he saw how difficult, if not impossible, it would be to separate the two friends. He tested Tom and found him full of the most ridiculous belief in the genuineness of Baretti. Mark did not doubt that Tom laid the flattering unction to his own soul in all sincerity.

'My cousin Tom,' said Mark to himself,
'is fool enough for anything.'

But in due time Baretti's picture was
finished and paid for, and, before its transfer
to my Lord Bellamy's country seat, was on
view at one of the Pall Mall galleries. It
made some noise in the world of art and
brought a commission or two.

On the day on which Baretti received his
cheque it happened that Mark and Tom sat
together in the latter's room. Enter the
painter in his dark purple velvet, his smoking
cap and slippers—a study in colour.

'Good-day, Mr. Mark Carroll!' cried the
little man, with a beaming countenance.
'Good-day, Mr. Tom Carroll!' He fluttered
the fortunate piece of paper in one hand and
executed a fantastic *pas seul.* 'That,' he said,
clapping the document on the table and
bringing down both palms upon it resonantly,
'is the cheque of my Lord Bellamy for three

hundred sterling pounds. Aha! It is addressed to Antonio Baretti, Esquire, and Antonio Baretti, Esquire, has written his famous name of European celebrity upon the back of it. Observe, Mr. Mark Carroll—until the famous name was written upon its back that document was without value. By inscribing the famous name I create three hundred sterling English pounds! I venerate myself like a cashier of the Bank of England. More. I pay my debts, and I kiss the hands of the best of men, my preserver.'

Before Tom had guessed what he was about, the painter was actually on his knees putting his words into action. The young Englishman blushed, and upset his chair in his haste to be out of gratitude's way. Mark looked on, smiling, with a smile that characterised the pair.

'Humbug and idiot!' said Mark's smile. Though Tom had run out of Baretti's way he looked at the little painter with gratified affection, plainly to be read through all his embarrassment. And in the fiery Italian's dark eyes there was a visible moisture.

'You be blowed!' said Tom, making a feeble shot at humour, and trying lamely to disguise his own pleasure. 'Who asked you for the money?'

'Not you,' said Baretti, with a happy and affectionate laugh. 'Not you by a word or a look. He lends,' he cried, turning to Mark, 'with the magnificence of Mæcenas, and he waits for repayment like Patience upon a pedestal.'

'He does,' cried Mark, his smile expanding. 'If he can't see through this,' thought Mark, 'the beggar's too blear-eyed to see through anything.'

'Rubbish!' said Tom. 'I'm very glad you have the money, Baretti, very glad. Pay me when you like.'

'I like to pay you now,' said Baretti.

' Not—believe me !—not that it is a burden to owe you money ' (Mark grinned outright at this touch of artful simplicity), ' but because to pay you is yet the greatest pleasure I have ever known.' Tom looked at Mark, and Baretti caught the glance. ' Your cousin,' he cried, ' is no stranger to this business. He knows what you lent me, and why you lent it.' Tom looked at him with reproach in his eyes. ' I could not help telling him,' said the artist beseechingly.

' I ought to have told you, Tom, how affectionately Mr. Baretti spoke of you,' said Mark, with commendable gravity. The acting on both sides was really diverting to Mark, who believed in Tom's annoyance just as much as in Baretti's gratitude.

' Rubbish ! ' said Tom, again.

' Sit down, Carroll,' cried Baretti, ' and write me a cheque for one hundred and fifty pounds.'

Tom, with a little air of lingering unwillingness, obeyed, and Baretti, having acquitted his debt, executed a second fantastic *pas seul.*

'Will they take so small a sum as this at the bank?' he demanded by-and-by. 'Then let us go and put it in straightway. Come! I will make myself fit for out-of-doors in a minute.'

He darted away, returning presently attired in a velvet shooting-coat and a wideawake hat, and drawing on, with loving care and precision, a pair of lavender-coloured kid gloves. He wore white gaiters over his little patent-leathered feet, and carried a natty little cane-stick under his arm.

Mark, having no especial business on his hands, accompanied Baretti and his cousin. Before they had gone a hundred yards they saw, in a quiet street opening off Montague Gardens, two people walking placidly towards them. The one was a stoutish, broad-shouldered young man, with a swarthy fat face, beady eyes, and a jetty moustache. On cheeks and chin he was blue with close shaving, and it was a hundred pounds to a penny, at first sight, that he was an operatic tenor and an Italian. The other was a gloriously-caparisoned young woman, a pronounced brunette, with large, languishing black eyes, and extremely ripe, red lips, and a languishing gait, which was yet elastic. Her figure was inclined, but only inclined, to *embonpoint*, and Mark, who thought himself something of a connoisseur in female beauty, pronounced her a fine woman on the spot. Baretti beholding the approaching pair, who walked arm-in-arm with a tender leaning towards each other, broke away from his companions and made a dash at the swarthy fat man, whom he hailed in voluble Italian and kissed vehemently on both cheeks, standing on tiptoe to do it. Next, with much ceremony, he saluted the lady, and the swarthy man was heard to murmur—

'Signora Malfi.'

'This,' said Baretti, turning to Tom and Mark, 'is my famous countryman—like my- self, of Naples—Signor Malfi. Il Maestro Thomas Carroll,' addressing the Italian.

'Rubbish!' said Tom, for the third time that morning, but he bowed to the swarthy Italian and the radiant young woman, whilst Baretti introduced cousin Mark. Cousin Mark, finding the stranger's stock of English extremely limited, addressed him in Italian (of which tongue he was complete master), thanking him, with many courteous flourishes, for the delight which he (the swarthy, fat man) had given Mark at Milan, and Naples, and in London. Signor Malfi took all this like a man who was used to it, but he was nevertheless pleased to find an Englishman to whom it was no trouble to talk, and he set out at once in the open street with a vivacious history of the villanies of one Corditi, a miserable wretch who presumed to consider himself a rival. All this was Italian to Tom, who was relieved when he saw Baretti shaking hands with the tenor and preparing to leave him. But there was still a little delay. The wickednesses of the rival tenor had made some explanations necessary to a provincial theatrical manager then in town, and Signor Malfi begged Baretti to accompany him and translate.

'Signor Baretti,' said Mark, in the operatic tenor's own tongue, 'is a busy man just now, and I am an idle one. I am entirely at your service.'

'You of the family of Carroll,' said the painter, 'are all alike. Generous and obliging to a fault.'

Mark smiled in answer. The Signora Malfi was a singularly fine woman, and Mark had nothing to do. And, besides, the briefless barrister was one of those men who always find it worth while to know theatric and

operatic people. One got stalls in that way
at times, and to a man who is bound to be
seen in the world, and who has no great
resources of his own, that sort of thing is
worth angling for. The singer was not un-
willing to accept Mark's good offices, and Mark
insisted on proffering them with almost over-
whelming politeness. So it befell that Baretti
and Tom went one way, whilst Mark and his
new acquaintances went another in pursuit
of the theatrical manager. The signora's face
and figure, and the signora's conversation, had
so many attractions for Mark that, when the
manager had been visited and the singer's
honour—on which he appeared to set some
value—had been cleared, he consented to dine
with his obliged friends, and accompanied
them to a restaurant in Prince's Street, where
garlic was the staple of half the dishes, and
the Chianti was excellent.

Here were other gentlemen with stoutish,

broad-shouldered figures, swarthy fat faces, beady eyes and jetty moustaches, who were also blue with close shaving on cheeks and chin. With most of these Signor Malfi was on easy terms, and they shouted from their different parts of the room, and gesticulated at each other with amiable ferocity across the little oblong tables on which the meal was served. The signora was the only person of the gentler sex there present, and Mark observed an absence of restraint in conversation which argued the lady of an indulgent turn.

After dinner the company drank coffee, clustered at one table, and smoked cigars, called Virginian, priced at twopence and measuring nine inches in length; and finally three or four of the swarthy fat men started with Signor Malfi and the lady for their apartments, Mark keeping them company still. All the men pausing in the middle of

Wardour Street to shout together, in the absurd belief that they were discussing something, Mark politely offered his arm to the signora, and at an easy pace walked on.

CHAPTER III.

THOMAS CARROLL the elder was a justice of the peace, and chairman of the guardians of the poor. He owned half a village and some two thousand acres of land in a Mid-England county.

To be a landowner is not, of itself, to be uncommon. A justice of the peace is not necessarily higher than the angels. There are chairmen of boards of guardians, even, who will never set the Thames on fire. But to be Thomas Carroll was, in the very nature of things, to be a remarkable man.

When people differed from Mr. Carroll, as they sometimes did, he displayed surprise and pity. In politics he was a Tory, and it was a habit of his to say that he could only conceive of a Radical as a fool or a knave. In either case he knew how to tolerate. A large nature is always lenient.

To have bought him at his own price and sold him in open market would have broken the Bank of England. In his affable way he condescended to everybody, and was mightily proud of having so little pride. As befitted his sense of his own majesty he was tall and portly. He was bald to the crown, and he came out in photographs as a man with a lofty forehead. His iron-gray hair was crisp and curled, his cheeks were rosy, his hands were large, and very plump and white. In dress he was a trifle old-fashioned, and he wore but one jewel, a big rose-diamond, which gave opportunities for the display of his handsome fingers.

Trench House, his residence, dominated Overhill and looked down upon it from a turfy, well-timbered slope which faced southward—a big, squat building in mellow red brick, not very picturesque, but looking homelike and dignified in the midst of its trees and lawns and gardens. Within easy view of its front windows there stood (and for that matter still stands) a gray old farmhouse, which was tenanted by a yeoman whose forbears had once owned the land about it. These people had fallen bit by bit from their prosperous estate, and had parted bit by bit with their possessions, and now for a generation or two they had farmed the land more or less unsuccessfully. One Michael Moore, the first of the family of whom any record had been kept, had been an Ironside. His sword and his iron head-pot were preserved in a high state of polish and glitter above the mantle-shelf. One George Moore had served two years in the county jail as a physical-force Chartist, and his memory was also cherished. The existent Michael Moore was proud of these bright spots in the family bead-roll, and was an uncompromising Radical. In the struggle for the repeal of the Corn Laws the existent Michael had made his name a stench in the nostrils of supporters of the agricultural interest, and had been looked upon as an Achan in the agricultural camp. He had had painted across the front of the farmhouse (so that his Tory landlord might read the legend whenever he looked out of window), 'Peace, Retrenchment, and Reform,' and the letters were dimly traceable even now. Perhaps if Michael had devoted himself to farming with the ardour he threw into politics he might have prospered.

On a certain misty autumn afternoon Mr. Carroll, mounted on a handsome hack, jogged comfortably along the road which led from Trench House to the farm, and sighted a little crowd about the building. Remembering suddenly the occasion of this gathering, he would fain have turned back again, but he knew that he must have been observed already, and so held on. The crowd was made up of the people of the village, with here and there a stranger, and standing in a waggon in front of the house with a table before him was a man in a white hat, who held forth noisily.

'Any advance on twelve ten? Twelve ten! A high-class heifer, sire and dam both known! Really, gentlemen, really! Thirteen? Thank you, Mr. Jones. Thirteen! Any advance on thirteen?'

The last link between the Moores and their old homestead was broken, and they were going away.

As Mr. Carroll, with raised hat in answer to many salutations from the farmyard, was jogging by, there came from the yard-gate a man with a florid complexion and white hair.

'So you've come to see the last of us, eh, Squire? You'll be easier in your mind when we're gone, no doubt.'

'I am afraid the village will not be sorry to lose you, Moore,' returned the landlord. 'But you will have the goodness to remember that this is none of my doing.' He waved his hand towards the yard, from which they were hidden by the corner of the building. 'I can but feel that I have been forbearing as a landlord, not merely in the matter of rent, but in respect also to the farm, which has considerably deteriorated in value of late years.'

'Well, Squire,' returned the other, 'you've little enough to grumble over. As to the rent, you'll have it to the uttermost farthing; and as to the farm, it's been treated better than it deserves. It's a sour, poor land, and always was, and always will be. But I don't want to have any bad blood between you and me.'

'My good fellow——' began Mr. Carroll, with a tolerant wave of his hand, and a smile of tranquil amusement.

'Whatever I've said again' you has been

said as a public duty, and not again' you as a
man,' pursued the farmer.

'You do me some injustice, Moore,' said
Mr. Carroll, with his tranquil smile. 'I don't
know what you have said; I don't care at all
what you have said. I am sorry to destroy
any dream you may have cherished, but it is a
fact that you have never troubled me, except
by your mismanagement of the land.'

'I know you're tough enough in the hide,'
said the farmer, 'but I thought I might have
pricked you once or twice. I don't think
you're a bad sort at bottom, though you'll find
out more than you know about the land when
you begin to farm it, as I'm told you're going
to. But I'm going away, and I want to do it
friend-like. I've got nothing again' you, Squire,
barring politics, and I'm not averse to shaking
hands, if so be that you are willing.'

'Very well, my good fellow,' said the
Squire, leaning downwards and proffering two

fingers of his right hand. The other two were needed to hold the gold-headed riding whip.

'I don't want two fingers, Squire,' said the outgoing tenant. 'I want a hand, if I have anything.'

'Very well, my good fellow, very well,' said Mr. Carroll again, smiling outright this time. 'I wish you well, Moore, and if you desire to give my good wishes effect, you will drop those foolish political notions of yours and give your time and your thoughts to business. A man in your station has no business with politics.'

'All right, Squire,' said the farmer. 'I've said already you're not a bad sort at bottom, and I'm glad there's no ill-blood between us. Good-bye!'

'Shall I see you again?' asked Mr. Carroll, with twinkling eyes and his clean-shaven lips twitching. Mr. Carroll was fond of musing on the subject of human egotism, and Moore's display tickled him rarely.

' No,' said the farmer. ' Woolley is lawyer as well as auctioneer, and he's got a full list of my debts. He'll pay 'em all; the rent among 'em. So this is good-bye in earnest.'

'Good-bye, Moore, good-bye! And take my advice about the politics.'

With that the Squire rode away, still calmly amused. It was noticeable that most men's estimates of Mr. Carroll tickled him. Almost everybody, with the exception of people of the lowest class, spoke to him as they spoke to any-body else! He had frequent cause to smile at human insolence, but to have been ruffled by it would have been too absurd. He jogged along in a splendid placid contentment until the rail-way station was in sight. At some expense to himself and some inconvenience to the vil-lage, he had insisted that the railway line should not approach his house too closely. It was a branch line and a small affair, which so far paid no dividend, and Mr. Carroll had become a large shareholder in it in order to save his property from desecration. A train was puffing along, lazily enough, the steam ascending on the heavy autumn air in straight columns and lingering about the fields. At the station door was the solitary fly the village boasted, and standing near, apparently giving directions to the driver about a heap of luggage, was Thomas Carroll the younger, in company with a small man who looked like a foreigner. Mr. Carroll put up his gold-rimmed double-eyeglasses to be sure of his son's identity, and rode forward.

'How do you do, Tom? How do you do? I had not expected you until to-morrow.'

'I said the twenty-second,' answered Tom.

'And this,' said Mr. Carroll, 'is the twenty-first. I had ordered Baker to meet you here with the carriage. The same unmethodical Tom as ever.'

'I wondered nobody was here,' said Tom with a laugh. 'Father, this is Signor Baretti. My father, Baretti.'

Mr. Carroll bowed in good-humoured con-descension.

'The—the artist?' he asked, putting up the gold-rimmed glasses.

'Yes,' said Tom. 'You remember his picture at the Academy? Saturn after his fall—with a line from Keats, "Deep in the shady sadness of a vale."'

'Deep in the shady sadness of her veil,' said Mr. Carroll. 'Of course. I remember distinctly. You are welcome to Overhill, Mr.—er——'

'Baretti,' said Tom.

'You are welcome to Overhill, Mr. Baretti,' said Tom's father, 'and welcome to Trench House. I am superior,' he added, with a charming smile and a reassuring wave of the right hand, 'to the absurd prejudices which animate so many members of my own class with regard to yours.'

Baretti bowed with commendable gravity, but there was a twinkle in his handsome Italian eyes which seemed to bespeak an inward sentiment of mirth.

' I thank you, sir,' he said, breaking silence for the first time.

' I am probably right in presuming,' said Mr. Carroll, with cheerful affability, ' that Mr. Baretti is not a native of this country? Ah, *Signor* Baretti! Of course—of course! An Italian, Signor Baretti?'

' I am an Italian, sir,' returned the painter.

' I know nothing more absurd than national prejudices,' said Mr. Carroll, genially. 'An Italian is as welcome at Trench House, Signor Baretti, as an Englishman. A man of large nature is cosmopolitan.'

Baretti bowed again, not feeling called upon to say anything. Tom hid his embarrassment among the luggage, and his father, with an expression of the pleasure it would give him to meet Tom's friend at dinner, rode on again.

'Take these things up to the house,' said Tom to the driver of the fly. 'We'll walk, Baretti.' The painter cheerfully assenting, they went on together. In a while Carroll turned upon his companion with a laugh half shy and half sly. 'Well, Baretti. Isn't he pretty nearly as good as I told you he would be?'

'I do not like,' said Baretti gravely, 'that a son should speak lightly of a father.'

'No, no,' cried the young Englishman, with a blush. 'He's a splendid old fellow, is my governor. I never knew a better man. But he *is* a little pompous. That's his only fault. He's a trifle pompous.'

'He *is* a little pompous,' Baretti assented with much gravity.

'But you mustn't be offended by him,' said Tom.

'I shall not be offended by him,' returned Baretti, with a look of almost canine affection at his companion.

'I wanted to walk,' said Tom, not without something of an air of haste to be rid of the subject, 'so that I might show you some of those ready-made pictures I spoke of. There! That old farmhouse is one of them, though this is an unfortunate day for looking at it, because the mist shuts out the distance. This is the real point of view, over the stile here. It's a little muddy, but a landscape painter in search of subjects won't mind that, I dare say.'

The landscape painter in search of subjects seemed to hang back a little. It was not the mud which made him linger, as Tom discovered when he turned. A girl with a graceful figure and attired like a lady came walking in the direction of the stile, most unaffectedly crying as she walked.

'Dear me, Miss Moore,' cried Tom, vaulting

into the field and approaching, hat in hand, 'you are in distress.'

The girl, in answer to this obvious statement, looked up and blushed and started, then paled and looked down again.

'I was saying good-bye to the old place, Mr. Carroll,' she answered, simply. 'I didn't know that anyone was near.'

'Are you going away?' asked Tom. 'We shall all be sorry to lose you.'

'Yes,' the girl answered, suppressing a fresh burst of tears. 'Everything was sold to-day, and we leave to-night.'

'God bless my soul!' said Tom, fatuously.

'The farm has not been paying for a long time,' the girl went on, 'and father resolved to sell everything and go to London.'

'To London?' asked Tom in amazement. 'What on earth is a farmer going to do in London? I beg your pardon, I didn't mean to be impertinent, but all this is such news to me.

'He means to start a dairy there,' the girl explained. 'Won't you go in, Mr. Carroll? He will be glad to see you.'

She mounted the stile without Tom's assistance, and pulling down her veil led the way to the house. Baretti had walked on a little, and Tom in passing asked to be excused for a minute. The farmer, with an unconcerned, if not a very cheerful look, sat by the fireside smoking. The room and the walls were bare, and the chamber wore a wretched and dismantled aspect.

'How d'ye do, Mister Thomas?' said the smoker, rising with a hearty greeting. 'Sit down, sir—sit down. There's nothing but the chimney-settle to sit on, for we're clearing out to-day, but you won't mind that, I know.'

'But what does it all mean?' asked Tom. 'Isn't it very sudden?'

'Sudden!' said the farmer, with a grim laugh. 'It began in _his_ day.' He looked upward to the spot on which the Cromwellian soldier's sword and head-piece had been used to hang. 'He owned the land, and he was the first that ever raised money on a foot of it. And, saving your presence, we've been going to the devil ever since, at greater or lesser speed, and—here we are.' He waved a hand to indicate the bare walls and floor, and laughed again. 'But at last, Mister Thomas, I've shook that four-hundred-acre incubus off the family shoulders, and I feel my own man again. The missis takes on at going, and so does Azubah, but I've done the right thing, and though it's a bit of a wrench when all's said, I'm glad I've done it.'

'Then there has been no quarrel with my father?' Tom asked.

'Your father!' said the farmer, with a much more cheerful laugh. 'I don't believe the Old Enemy himself could quarrel with your father, sir. He'd no more dream of quarrelling

with me than I should of harbouring a deadly
spite again a mouse. He's too lofty for it. I
put it to him this afternoon, scarce an hour
ago : " There's no ill-blood betwixt us, Squire?"
says I. Why, I saw him laughing at me, at
the bare idea of my having the cheek to think
I was big enough for him to think about.'

'Come, come, Moore,' said Tom, in a tone
of remonstrance.

'Oh, that's your duty, sir, and I'll say no
more!' returned the farmer. 'And I'm glad to
know you come in time to see the last of us.
The two houses, so they do say, fowt on different sides in Cromwell's time, but we've been
good friends and neighbours since, and I'm
pleased to part at peace. Well, sir, here's the
cart at the door, and we've got the train to
catch. It's a short welcome for the last time,
Mister Thomas, but it'll always be a good one
so long as there is a roof-tree over Michael
Moore's head. So, good-bye, sir, and God bless

you!' He shook hands with Tom, wringing his hand harder than he knew, and bustled to the foot of the stairs. 'Here's Jack ready with the cart, missis, and Mister Thomas is here to say good-bye.'

The farmer's daughter stood in the middle of the dismantled room, and Tom Carroll, looking at her, felt grieved for her. He had played with her when he was a child, and he had known her all his life.

'I am sorry you are going,' he said; 'very sorry.' He held out his hand, and she laid hers in it languidly. He felt a little awkward and clumsy at this, for he had meant a farewell shake-hands, and the girl's fingers gave no sign of a responsive grip. So he stood feeling foolish enough for perhaps ten seconds, and that, though not a long time in most circumstances, is more than long enough to feel foolish in with any degree of comfort. In spite of his discomfiture, however—and he was always shy with women—he could not help looking at his old playmate, and it came into his mind with something of a shock—what a pretty girl she was! Not in the conventional way, perhaps, but what splendid soft brown eyes, what a sensitive mouth, how graceful a figure, what a pretty curve in the neck and shoulders, while the sad head drooped and the brown eyes looked up tearful and artless like a child's! Yet the girl was eighteen if she were a day, and old enough to have known better than to look at a young man in a fashion so embarrassing if only she had thought about it. It was sufficiently evident that she thought of nothing just then except the sorrow of going and parting, unless it were, perhaps, the altogether unacknowledged and unconscious comfort of having her hand in a friend's, and that friend a man.

Whatever embarrassment the situation held was on Tom's side only, for Tom was conscious, and the girl was not. A step and a voice at the door promised relief, but in effect made matters serious.

'Azubah,' cried a young lady, entering suddenly, 'how dare you try to go away like this without letting me know of it?' The new-comer kissed the girl exuberantly, and made a sweeping curtsey to Tom, who blushed fierily and fidgeted with his hands and feet. It was noticeable that until the entrance of this new figure the farmer's daughter had worn a look of pretty refinement and delicacy; but in the radiance of the new-comer, and by contrast with her exquisite finery, the girl's pretti-ness dwindled into plainness, her refinement took an immediate rusticity, and her dress looked poor. Nobody would have said that the new-comer was over-dressed, but every-thing she wore was rich and fashionable, and she herself had the art of wearing clothes to perfection, and she moved and looked like a princess—like a princess in a tale, that is, and not absolutely like the real thing, which is sometimes (treasonable as it may sound to say it) dowdy.

'I wrote to you, Miss Lording,' said the farmer's daughter, 'and sent the letter to the post an hour ago.'

'You are a wicked girl,' returned Miss Lording, kissing her again vehemently. 'And as for you, Mr. Moore,' turning to the farmer, 'I think you most unkind to allow Azubah to go away without saying good-bye to me.'

'Now come, Miss Lording,' said Moore, with a jocose and waggish air, '*you* ought to know better than to say that. You know what sort of a life you lead *your* father, a-riding rough-shod over all his orders, and I know what sort of life my girl leads me. When I'm as dead as paternal authority is, I shall be ripe for burying.'

'Here is another criminal,' Miss Lording

said, turning severely towards Tom. 'You might have told me, Mr. Carroll.'

'Like yourself, Miss Lording,' said Tom, 'I only learned the news this afternoon. I have just arrived from town.'

'Where are you going, Azubah?' asked the young lady.

'We're all going up to London, miss,' said the farmer, 'and Azubah will doubtless write to say, when we're settled, where we are. But here's the missis, and the cart's waiting, and it's good-bye all round.'

He shook hands with overdone bustle, and flourished his hat at the door behind his departing wife and daughter, leaving his guests behind him. Perhaps in spite of the gaiety of his manner he was aware of something in his eyes which might have told how the old farmer felt on uprooting himself from the soil on which his yeoman ancestors had grown and flourished. The latest comer followed, holding up her skirts from the dusty floor and the bedraggled yard; and Tom, hat in hand, went after. The farmer bustled the women into the dog-cart, mounted in turn, took the reins, and drove off. His wife and daughter, who faced backward on the old place they were leaving, began to cry, and to wave pocket-handkerchiefs in token of farewell. Miss Lording and Tom responded, and when the cart had passed the corner of the lane the lady turned to her carriage, which stood at the farmyard gate, in charge of an old coachman of extremely grave and responsible aspect. In place of ascending, as Tom expected, she turned back again.

'I am sorry,' she said, ' to have interrupted your leave-taking, Mr. Carroll, but,' she added, with a shrug of the shoulders and a dazzling smile, 'the door was open, and it was not my fault.'

'Don't mock me always,' Tom besought her, miserably.

She laughed outright and clapped her hands.

'You looked deliciously sentimental, Mr. Carroll. Is that a friend of yours? Who is he? He looks odd and attractive, and as if he were somebody.'

'My friend Baretti, the artist,' said Tom.

'Baretti!' she answered. 'Was it he who painted Saturn? "Deep in the shady sadness of a vale." Oh, Tom, I am sorry I teased you! And you always do know such nice people. Bring him here.'

Tom bowed delightedly, and ran after Baretti.

'I want to introduce you to Miss Lording, Baretti,' he said when he came up with him. 'She wants to know you. Your Academy picture impressed her greatly.'

They returned together, and the little artist being presented, the queenly young lady said many pleasant things to him, and finally drove

away, leaving the two young men standing in
the lane with the mist closing about them, and
feeling very much as if a summer sun had suddenly vanished from the skies, carrying all his
warmth and brightness with him.

'Carroll,' said the painter a minute later, in
his vehement Italian way, 'I have beheld my
ideal of all feminine grace and beauty. What
splendour! what grace! what charm!'

'Yes,' said Tom, in an oddly grudging way.
'She's very pretty, isn't she?'

'*Gran Dio!*' cried the painter, casting his
arms wildly upwards. 'He professes to have a
soul, and he calls that vision of beauty—very
pretty!'

CHAPTER IV.

Mr. Carroll the elder and Mr. Carroll the younger sat together that evening after dinner. Baretti had retired ostensibly to write letters, but really with no other object than to leave father and son alone to talk over any matters they might have in mind after a separation of a month or two.

'And what are you doing with yourself in London, Tom?' asked the father, sipping at his wine.

'Fiddling,' said Tom, lightly, 'painting, writing.'

'Things have changed since my day,' said Mr. Carroll, not without a tinge of sorrow in his tones. 'The occupations of which you speak are now the recognised relaxations of a gentleman. I suppose the change is a part of that progress of which we hear so much, and though I am far from admiring it, I can see it is far beyond individual control. You belong to your new generation and I belong to my old one, and we shall not convince each other.' He sighed complacently, and drawing a gold snuff-box from his pocket, tapped it, opened it, closed it again, and put it back without using it. This was a habit with him. It probably comforted him with some old-world notions of a time when gentlemen had distinctive little customs of their own, which had not descended to the lower classes. 'There are some practices,' he resumed, 'which are likely to be conserved even in these days of social decadence. And—apropos,' he added with a smile, 'when do you think of getting married?'

Somewhat to the elder man's surprise the younger one blushed at this query.

'I'm glad you've mentioned that subject, father,' said Tom with a smiling embarrassment.

'Aha!' said Mr. Carroll with stately geniality. 'Who is the lady?'

'Well,' said Tom, blushing more deeply, 'I have seen a good deal of her in town, and we have known each other a long time, and— it's Miss Lording. I haven't said a word about it until now, but——'

'You think you understand each other?' asked the father.

'No,' cried Tom. 'I don't think she dislikes me—but——'

'Miss Lording,' said Mr. Carroll, producing the gold snuff-box again and going once more through his pretence of preparation. 'Miss Lording is a young lady who would ornament any sphere and do credit to any household. She is handsome, well-bred, well-connected, and well to do.' Tom's diffidence did not extend itself to his father, and the elder man's estimate of Miss Lording as his son's future wife was in a second loftier than any opinion of her he had previously held. When anything or person became in any way an appanage to the splendours of Thomas Carroll the elder, it was beautified at once by the halo which to his own eyes always dwelt upon him. 'I am growing a little tired,' he continued, 'of my duties as justice of the peace, and when you are married and settled down I shall be glad to see you succeeding to your father's functions. I have fulfilled that duty now for a quarter of a century, not altogether without credit.'

'I am glad to have your approval,' said Tom, bashfully. It was difficult as yet to talk even to his father on such a matter.

'Your mention of that topic leads me,' said Mr. Carroll, 'to a subject of some importance which affects myself. When I asked you to bring down your artistic friend, I did so with a purpose. You spoke very highly of him, and I am told that in regard to such matters your judgment is to be trusted. When a gentleman undertakes a public duty he does not look for a reward, but it is possible that either by length of service or by the exercise of an unusual ability he may secure some recognition. I have received a letter signed on behalf of my colleagues on the Bench by Lord Bellamy. In that letter I am informed that at a recent meeting of the county justices it was unanimously resolved—unanimously resolved—to invite me to sit for my portrait to any artist of my choice. It is proposed to preserve the picture,' he added with composed magnificence, 'in the Shire Hall itself. The act, as you will observe, is spontaneous, and I will not disguise the fact that it is of a nature calculated to gratify me.'

'Assuredly,' said Tom ; 'a very high compliment indeed.' He was not quite as well pleased with the news as if it had come at another moment.

'Your friend Baretti is thoroughly competent to the task?' inquired Mr. Carroll.

'Competent!' cried Tom. And he began to praise Baretti much beyond his merits, which were great. His father being willing, the enthusiast ran to his friend's room and brought him downstairs. Baretti began at once to regard Mr. Carroll with a critical and observant eye, and to move about him so as to get various views of him, insomuch that the subject began to think the artist disrespectful.

'I have never found time to devote myself to the study of the fine arts,' said Mr. Carroll, by-and-by, 'although I am not one of those who regard a knowledge of the minutiæ of those pursuits as being unworthy of a gentleman. But my interest, although it has found but a casual expression, has been consistent, and I have often thought that when one calls to mind the gratification it affords to future generations to look upon the lineaments of one who has been esteemed in his day and generation, one is tempted to invest the portrait-painter with an almost factitious importance, and to identify him with his theme.'

'Yes,' said Tom, with a laugh, 'one may say more than that sometimes. Look at that glorious collection of portraits of old nobodies at the Musée Plantin. I dare say somebody knows their histories, but if Rubens hadn't painted them nobody would have cared to know whether they had lived or died.' He had said all this in one eager burst, before he had time to think that it was not quite complimentary to his father. 'You must do your best to immortalise my father, Baretti,' he added, uncomfortably.

This view of the case was new to Mr. Carroll, but it was his habit to ignore things which seemed to work against his own conceptions of himself. He looked at Tom with an allowing smile, but gave no further expression to his thoughts. People frequently had opinions of that sort, and it was scarcely worth while to interrupt them. He put the finger-tips of both hands together, and addressed Baretti, as if unconscious of the interruption.

'It is unfortunate that our list of reliable portraits of eminent men is so small. We have, for instance, no reliable representation of the greatest of English poets. And when one reflects that it was within the power of any inconsiderable number of inconsiderable people to offer to him such a requisition as that of which I am the honoured recipient, one is the more regretful and the more surprised.' Mr. Carroll warmed with this theme, and continued: 'What would we give for a portrait of King Solomon, a reliable likeness of Alexander, of Bruce, or of Alfred the Great?' Nobody offering to appraise the value of these lost blessings, he paused awhile, and then, rising from his seat, unlocked a drawer and took from it Lord Bellamy's letter. He put up his gold eye-glasses and read it through, holding it at arm's-length; then, folding it, he resumed his seat, and, tapping the paper against the eye-glasses, and gazing serenely at the fire, he said, ' I shall certainly accede to the request of my fellow-justices.'

The talk drifted, and no further allusion was made to Tom's matrimonial prospects. The young fellow, who was not much of an egotist, and never very disposed to be exigent about his own affairs, felt yet a little hurt at the fashion in which his father had shelved the theme. An only son's marriage might have seemed, he thought, at least as interesting as even the flattering request of the county justices. Tom went to bed a little depressed and disheartened, but the topic near his heart found a renewal next morning.

Breakfast was just over. Mr. Carroll was reading the 'Times.' Tom was standing at the fire, and Baretti was in another room, setting up an easel and generally preparing for the beginning of the new commission, when a knock sounded on the door of the breakfast-room. Tom called, 'Come in,' and a servant entered, bearing a card upon a salver.

'Show Mr. Lording this way, Johnson,' said Mr. Carroll. 'Your arrival is auspicious, Lording.'

'I am glad to hear it,' said the new-comer. He threw back a pair of broad shoulders and showed a set of white teeth as he laughed. 'Polly saw Master Tom yesterday, and I've just come round to see him. How's London, Tom? And how's the *magnum opus*, the Opera? And why is my arrival auspicious, Carroll? Eh?'

There was nothing surprisingly comic in this speech, but the speaker laughed so heartily after it that he might have uttered the happiest of *bons mots* and been less pleased.

'Sit down,' said Mr. Carroll, 'and I will tell you.'

'Gad!' said the visitor, sitting down, 'you look as solemn as if Calcraft wouldn't act, and they wanted me to play the part of sheriff in good earnest! What's the matter?'

'It's scarcely so terrible as that,' said Tom, who felt sure of the father, at least, whatever the daughter's opinions might prove to be.

'The fact is, Lording,' said Mr. Carroll, addressing himself to his visitor with a ponderous gravity, 'Tom and I were last night discussing a matter of the utmost moment to his welfare. I had asked him—without any expectation of a definite answer—whether he had as yet any ideas upon the marriage question. To my surprise, he mentioned your daughter.'

'Eh?' said the old gentleman. 'Why,

she's a baby! And you're no more than a boy, Tom!'

'I am five-and-twenty,' said Tom defensively.

'Then, by Jove!' said Lording, 'she's more than nineteen, for you weren't six when she was born. Gad, how time flies! eh, Carroll?'

Mr. Carroll regarded his guest with an eye which seemed to convey a tolerant rebuke to flippancy.

'I should have approached you with more ceremony——' he began.

'Ceremony be hanged!' cried Lording. 'I never was more surprised in my life. But if Tom wants the girl to marry him he must ask her. And if she will, she must; and if she won't, it's of no use to ask me to do anything. And I wish you luck, my lad, and I hope, if the little girl says yes, that you'll be happy.'

'The match would meet with your good-
will?' inquired Mr. Carroll.

'Seriously,' said the guest, with a visage
suddenly grown solemn, 'I am pleased and
proud.' He laughed a second later. 'What
sort of luck you may have—Tom, my lad—
I can't even guess. But I dare say, you rascal,
you know all about that already. Eh?'

'Indeed, sir!' Tom began in tones of
protest.

'You don't?' cried Miss Lording's father.
'Gad, sir, your old dad and I knew our way
about a little better than you youngsters seem
to do. Didn't we, Carroll?' He threw back
his square grey head and his big shoulders,
and laughed prodigiously, and made a motion
to dig Mr. Carroll in the ribs.

'I am happy,' said that gentleman, evading
Lording's fingers, and speaking with much
gravity of manner, 'that the proposal meets
with your approval.'

'Well,' said the guest, beaming, 'it's a matter for Polly to settle, I suppose, and if she says yes, I don't see who's to prevent it.'

There was a knock at the door. 'Come in,' cried Tom. 'My friend Baretti, Mr. Lording.'

'Good Lord!' cried the old gentleman, with another great laugh. '*Absit omen! Absit omen!* Glad to meet you, Mr. Baretti. My daughter spoke of having met you with my friend Tom here, and I promised myself the pleasure of making your acquaintance. I'm a plain countryman, Mr. Baretti, of the old school. I don't know much about art, but I have the sense to reverence, even where I haven't the brains to understand. My daughter is a judge of that sort of thing, and speaks of you in such terms, sir, that I am proud to meet you.'

He kept the artist's hand in his during the whole of this address, and when he had finished he laughed with much heartiness, though what (except his own high spirits) he had to laugh at what was not obvious.

'Mr. Baretti,' said the master of the house, 'has been so good as to consent to paint my portrait.'

'I did not know,' said the Italian, 'that you were engaged. I came to say that I was ready.'

'You don't mind my looking on?' asked Lording, with boylike eagerness. 'I've never seen anybody painting except my daughter. I suppose, now,' he asked, 'you paint in oils, don't you?'

'In this case,' said the artist, 'yes.'

'Is this the picture for the Shire Hall?' asked Lording.

'The picture for the Shire Hall,' assented Mr. Carroll, with tranquil majesty. 'The present,' he added, 'is the only time at our disposal. We will begin now, Mr. Baretti, if you please.'

Mr. Carroll, being marshalled by his three attendants to the room assigned, was set in a proper light, and being bidden to turn his head a little in such a way, and to lower his chin a little in such a way, to fold his hands in such a manner, and to settle his shoulders in such another manner, was a spectacle the like of which, for lordly condescension and regal obedience, is not often to be seen. The little Italian prowled around him with stealthy step and watchful eye, taking note of his proportions and his lines, and looked so much at the moment like some velvet beast of prey about to spring that Mr. Carroll experienced uncomfortable sensations.

'Is not the canvas rather small?' inquired the sitter.

'All the portraits in the Shire Hall are kit-cats,' answered Tom. 'This is the same size.'

'Kit-cats!' said Mr. Carroll, as if he tasted

the word and disapproved of its flavour; 'what is meant by kit-cats?'

'Sit still, if you please,' cried the painter. 'Now,' a moment later, 'you can move as much as you like.'

The sitter was silent, if only from sheer amazement. A minute or two later he laughed.

'You gentlemen of the brush,' he said, 'have something of a royal way with you when at work.'

'My sitters have told me that before,' said Baretti. The rebuke passed over his head. Mr. Carroll began to dislike the little man and his ways.

Lording looked on with great interest whilst Baretti painted, and Tom bore himself as well as he could, though he felt a little sore at the neglect of his affairs. In about two hours' time Baretti, who painted with great rapidity, had upon the canvas a foggy semblance of his sitter's form and features, with a sort of mud halo about the head.

'That will do for to-day,' he said, throwing down his brushes and stretching himself. 'The fire is out.'

Mr. Carroll rose solemnly and inspected the work. 'Do you detect a likeness, Lording?' he asked doubtfully.

'It's wonderful,' said Lording, 'really wonderful!' He turned to Baretti with almost an air of reverence: 'My girl paints very pretty in water-colours,' he said, 'but I never saw anyone paint in oils before. It's really very remarkable—very remarkable!'

'You set me at liberty for the rest of the day, Mr. Baretti?' demanded Mr. Carroll stiffly.

'Yes,' said the little painter, languidly; 'while the fire is alight I work. When it goes out I have done. I could not do anything more to-day even at a portrait.'

'Why *even* at a portrait?' asked Lording.

'Oh,' said the little man, lighting a cigar, 'a portrait is not often so—what is your word? —so demanding?—no—that will not do—a portrait does not often draw you on like a picture of your own choosing. You can put it away without sorrow, and you can work at it without joy.'

This as relating to portraits in general might be true enough, but Mr. Carroll began to have the meanest opinion of the painter's intellect.

'Well,' cried Lording, with another of his great laughs at the end of the statement, 'I've a ride before me, and something to do when I get home. Eh, Tom? Ha-ha-ha! You come over this afternoon, Tom, will you? Eh? Ha-ha-ha-ha! Good-morning, Tom! Good-morning, Carroll! Good-morning, Mr. Baretti! I'm very proud to have made your acquaintance, sir. See you this afternoon, Tom. Ha-ha-ha-ha-ha!'

He went out in a storm of merriment and Mr. Carroll retired with him, leaving Tom and Baretti together. Tom, with a flutter at his breast, went out of the room to avoid the necessity for talking, and the painter sat still for a time and smoked. But by-and-by he displaced the canvas from which Mr. Carroll's ghostly presentment stared at him, and set upon the easel a small panel on which he began to sketch with a bit of charcoal, touching here and there with such a wandering hand than an onlooker might have been puzzled to guess the meaning of the lines. But in a few minutes these lines all began to grow together, and in a few minutes more they resulted in a beautiful feminine face. The artist having regarded it attentively took up a duster, rubbed out the drawing, and began again. This time the beautiful feminine face came out as Miss Mary Lording's undoubted image, and the painter, resuming his seat, smoked tranquilly as he regarded it with half-shut, meditative eyes.

About five minutes later a step sounded in the corridor, and a hand was laid upon the handle of the door. The painter rose and rubbed the beautiful feminine face from the panel, almost with a feeling of detected guilt. He would have been troubled to guess why he had destroyed the drawing, and perhaps still more troubled to say why he felt guilty, but the face had been haunting him oddly ever since he had seen it, and was present in his mind with a curiously irresistible demand to be reproduced in visible form.

The intruder was the master of the house, and he, after one questioning look about the room, bowed in silence and retired. Baretti listened to his footsteps as they travelled towards Tom's chamber, which was in the same corridor, and then began to sketch anew. The same face came out upon the panel, and

once more he dusted it away, and this time
with a look of resolution, as if he had done
with the theme; he put away the panel and
set up the damp-gleaming ghostly presentation
of his host again. Then he walked restlessly
about the room, and next sat down at the table
and began to sketch the view from the window; but his thoughts strayed off, and, before
he knew it, there was a pretty hat in outline on
the paper, and below the hat a charming face
with an escaping curl or two upon the forehead
—Mary Lording to the life again. He tore the
paper with an exclamation of impatience and
left the room.

Now this might mean a good deal or it
might mean nothing—nothing, that is, but an
artistic fancy and an artistic preoccupation.
Ardent young artists are wont to be haunted
by shapes of beauty, and Baretti was likelier
to be impressed by form and colour than
another man. But artists are a good deal

hardened, too, in the matter of feminine charms, which, in their case, strike the eye with singular vividness, but leave the heart untouched; and if a painter fell in love with all the owners of the beautiful faces that dwell in his memory and ask to be painted, he would have his hands full. Yet the little Italian went about perturbed in spirit, and thought more of Mary Lording's face than was good for him.

Tom left him alone after luncheon, with no explanation of his errand, and Baretti made more sketches of random themes. The face crept into them all, and at last he resigned himself to the pleasure it gave him. His hand became so familiar with it, and his memory preserved it so clearly, that he drew it in all the varying expressions he had seen upon it until he began to long to give it colour, and yielded to the longing. Before twilight fell he had painted a delicate little picture in water-colour, slight, but very true and fine, and after staring at this until he could see it no longer, he put it away in his portmanteau and burned all the pencil sketches he had made.

CHAPTER V.

PAPA LORDING, riding home in the brisk air and sunlight, turned over in his mind the proposal young Carroll had made for his daughter's hand. He was a bluff and hearty man of a type common amongst English country gentlemen; had a rare good heart, a magnificent digestion, and as much mental polish as the fibre of which he was made would carry. He sucked marrow of mirth and laughter out of things at which most people do not even smile, and this was not because he was a humorist, but because his nature was of that downright sunlit sort which is probably only to be found among Englishmen. He had not the remotest idea as he rode that he was going to be involved in a love story at all out of the common. Here was a handsome young fellow, well connected and well-to-do, who had taken a liking in the ordinary fashion to a charming young woman of nineteen, also well connected and well-to-do. The pair would probably be married, and papa Lording would very well have liked, in the manner of his own earlier day, to have danced at the wedding.

The old gentleman confessed to himself, as he had confessed to the suitor an hour or two before, that he was without voice in the matter. His daughter drove him, and if it were only with a peacock's feather for whip, and a thread of silk for rein, he was none the less bound to go the way she wanted.

At the sound of hoof-beats in the avenue, Miss Lording ran from the room in which she sat into the hall, and there awaited her father. Rival charms are rarely so equally balanced that some girl or other has not the right to be called the belle of her part of the country, or the beauty of her county. Miss Lording had that right, and was probably aware of it. She was undeniably English in style (the loveliest style, as I make bold to believe, in the world) ; she had lovely eyes, a face of charming contour and expression, a wealth of hair of fine texture and glossy hue (her own), and a figure neither too ripe nor too fragile, too tall nor too dumpy. Her vivacity of spirit lit up those beautiful eyes with a constant variety of expression, and set that charming figure in a constantly varied and delicately graduated series of postures, so that she avoided all seeming of monotony without running into that opposing sin of jerkiness which is the snare of many lively young ladies, who, without it, might be charming.

Her father, having dismounted, surrendered his horse and ran up the stone steps which led to the hall. His genial British face and genial

British heart were alike aglow, and alike a
little tenderer than common. There was not
much romance in the good old gentleman's
nature, but the love stories of the young sometimes awaken memories in the minds of the
middle-aged, and he had been thinking on his
ride, with unwonted warmth and gentleness, of
the days of his own youth, when he himself
went a-courting. So the kiss which commonly
celebrated his return from an absence of whatever brevity was multiplied into three, one for
the dimple on each ripe cheek, and one for the
charming lips between them.

'Polly,' said the old gentleman, with twinkling eyes, 'I have brought a little present
for you.'

'Yes!' said the young lady, 'what is it?'
Her father, with one arm round her waist, led
her to the room she had quitted a moment
before, and there turning round faced her
squarely. 'What is the matter, papa?' she

asked. 'Why do you look at me so oddly?'

'Well,' said papa, 'the present I have to offer you (and it isn't mine) is an article which is supposed by good judges to be worth a great deal. I have seen such a thing described in print as a perfect mine of jewels. I've been told that it's a sort of talisman to make a good girl happy all her life long, provided that she doesn't lose it. I've actually known one or two cases in which it has really done as much. But, all the same, I'm not quite certain whether you'll care to have it.'

'You mustn't be a ridiculous old gentle-man,' said his daughter. 'What is it, dear?'

Perhaps in a general way she guessed the nature of the proffered gift, for she blushed slightly.

'It's a young man's heart, my darling,' said the old fellow, 'warranted sound and whole, and rising five-and-twenty.'

Miss Lording began to take a close and serious interest in the pattern of papa's watch-chain.

'Has the young man a tongue as well as a heart, papa?' she asked. 'And should I know his face if I saw it?'

'You'll see it this afternoon,' said the old gentleman, 'and then you can judge for yourself.'

'Am I to say "Yes" or "No" at once?' she asked, looking up at him saucily. 'Or may I wait until I see the heart's owner?'

'You had better wait,' he said, patting her cheeks affectionately. His voice was husky at that moment, for he saw quite suddenly a house that looked most mournful and empty, and himself going about it, solitary. The girl answered to his thoughts.

'Send the young man's heart back again, papa. It is no honest gift, but a bait.'

'Don't you ask to know whose it is?' he demanded.

'Young men don't give their hearts away for nothing,' said Miss Lording, still busy with her father's watch-chain. 'The young man has designs, and I have penetration enough to guess them. Send the wicked present back again, papa. I am happy without it.'

'Don't you ask to know whose it is?' he asked again.

'No,' she said, in a tone of mighty indifference, and wound the watch-chain about one of her white fingers with an air of elaborate interest.

'Very well, my dear,' said the old boy with a sigh. 'If it isn't to-day it will be to-morrow. The poor lad will be here this afternoon to take his present back again—a little cracked, I'm afraid.'

'Who is it, papa?' she asked.

'I thought you didn't want to know, you rogue!' cried her father with a laugh.

'But I have a right to know, sir, if I

choose,' she answered, with a pretty mock defiance.

'It's young Carroll,' said her father 'I shall have to give you away to somebody some day, and I could part with you to him as willingly as to anybody.' The girl was blushing, and even trembling a little, by this time. 'But if it's settled, and you won't have anything to say to him——' Some slight change in her posture, something in the droop of the head, perhaps, or something in the nervous action of the fingers toying with the watch-chain, stopped him. 'Is it "Yes" or "No," my dear?' he asked, putting an arm about her neck.

'I don't know, papa,' murmured the young lady.

'Well, well,' said the old gentleman, 'think it over, my dear, and decide for your own happiness.' He kissed her and left her a little sadly, feeling somewhat like a criminal whose repeal has been granted and snatched away again. 'These youngsters,' he said to himself, with half a sigh and half a laugh, 'come gaily enough to steal an old man's treasure. But Tom's a good lad—a good lad.'

Girls are known to be quick at sounding the affections of young people of the opposite sex when the affections concern themselves, and it is likely that Miss Lording was not very surprised at hearing Tom Carroll's name at the end of her father's little parable. There was nothing to dislike in the young man. He was tall and straight, and handsome and well-bred. He was reputed for a good-hearted fellow, and he was popular with all sorts and conditions of men. It would not be difficult to like him very much.

Now, this is not the language of ardent passion, but (Juliet and all manner of poetic precedents to the contrary notwithstanding) ardent passion is not altogether a pretty thing in a young woman to begin with. There are plenty of exceptions, of course, but the ordinary marriageable love of the ordinary marriageable young Englishwoman begins with liking and goes on in tranquil growth, finding deep root without the influence of storm, and learning to flourish, fair and calm and broad, in a tolerably equable temperature.

Whether his daughter were as yet in love with Tom Carroll or not, whether she simply liked him, or had already passed over the boundary line between liking and loving, was a problem too delicate for a man of papa Lording's blunt discernment to solve. But he felt pretty sure that the girl would say 'Yes' to Tom's question, and he was lonely in anticipation. The time seemed to drag with him until the lover came. Tom Carroll's heart beat higher than usual as he rode along the trim avenue, and surrendered his horse at the door. The old boy received him with more than common cordiality.

'I know nothing about it, Tom,' he said, 'but you have my best wishes. I don't authorise you to tell her so, mind, for she must make her own choice quite freely.'

'I understand you perfectly, sir,' said the youngster, a little proudly. 'I don't think I should care to marry any woman, however dearly—however highly I might esteem her, unless she took me of her own free will.'

'Quite right, Tom,' said the other; 'a very proper spirit. But don't you think you'd rather—have it over?'

'Why, yes, sir,' said Tom, with a dry little laugh, 'I should like to know.'

'Come this way,' said Lording, and Tom followed into a small, cheerfully-furnished sitting-room, in which Mary sat alone, making busy pretence of doing something with a needle. 'Tom has ridden over, my dear,' said her father, with a most transparent pretence of having nothing on his mind.

'Ridden over to have a look at us. I'll just leave him here for a minute whilst I go and——'

He had no excuse ready, and therefore slid away without one, leaving the young people together.

'Have you deserted your friend, Signor Baretti, Mr. Carroll?' asked the young lady.

'Yes,' said Tom, hurriedly plunging *in medias res*. 'I have come over with a very special object. I do not know whether your father has spoken of it.'

'A special object?' said the young lady, surveying her labours with a head set sideways, and an air of exasperating want of interest in his communication.

'I can't hope to tell you how much in earnest I am,' said Tom, 'or how much depends to me upon this interview.' He paused and looked at her. She was surveying her needle-work again with eyes of elaborate innocence, and he felt discouraged. 'I am here,' he went on desperately, 'to ask you to be my wife.'

Miss Lording bent over the elegant trifle upon her lap and gave it a yet closer scrutiny. Tom waited, and she said nothing. The silence began to grow extremely awkward. Some young men in an enterprise of this kind are easily abashed, and Tom Carroll was one of them. The longer the silence continued the harder it was to break it, and he felt cold and miserable.

'Have you no answer for me?' he said at last.

'I don't know,' said the young lady demurely, 'until—I am asked.'

Tom Carroll marched across the little room, planted a chair by her side, and sat down in it with an air of resolve.

'Will you?' he asked in a whisper—'will you be my wife?'

'Don't you think, Mr. Carroll,' she answered,

picking up the bit of needlework to examine it more closely, ' don't you think that this is a little—precipitate ? '

' Why,' cried Tom, ' we have known each other all our lives ! '

' I have not had any experience in such matters,' said the young lady, ' but I have always understood that there were preliminaries to a question of that sort.'

' Oh,' said the youngster, ' don't jest with me, Miss Lording ! Don't laugh at me ! It is death to me if it is sport to you.' He took the needlework trifle from her and possessed himself of her hands. ' Tell me,' he murmured.

' What ? ' demanded the disingenuous young woman, with averted countenance.

' Tell me you love me.'

' For shame, Mr. Carroll, to ask a poor girl to say such things ! '

' Will you be my wife ? ' said Tom, growing bolder every moment.

' I don't know,' she answered.

' You don't know how I love you,' said the courtier, with a hand in each of his.

' No,' she said, ' that is true. I have never been told.'

' Shall I tell you ? ' said he.

' Thank you,' she answered, with infinite dry demureness, ' I should like to hear it very much.'

' I can't,' said Tom. ' There are no words for it. I love you with all my heart and soul —but that seems to say nothing. I think,' he went on, blushing and stammering, ' that you are the most beautiful woman in the world.'

' That is very nice of you,' said Miss Lording, tranquilly. She was so exasperating that, though he never knew how it came about, Tom took her in his arms and kissed her over and over again. Perhaps that was the true way with her, and in any case (even if it were not that masterly method of wooing that won her) it was then that she was won.

'For shame, Mr. Carroll!' she cried, with face and neck and ears all rosy with blushes; 'it is well to have a giant's strength, but tyrannous to use it like a giant. Let me go.'

'Not until you promise,' cried the lover. 'Will you be my wife?'

'If you insist upon it,' said the young lady. 'But a promise under compulsion is no promise.'

Tom released her, and dropped upon one knee before her like a wooer of old days.

'Will you promise now?' She bent over him with mirth and tenderness.

'Do you wish it very much?' she asked.

'With all my soul,' he answered, taking her hands again. 'Will you promise?'

'You will be good?' she demanded.

'As gold,' said the young man.

'Then release me.' He dropped her hands,

still kneeling before her, and she took a step backward. 'I promise,' she said, and, whisking the door open, she skimmed from the room like a swallow, leaving her lover with hands that grasped at air. But the young fellow rose with a glad heart and went in search of his divinity's father.

'What news, Tom?' the old fellow asked.

'She accepts me, sir,' said Tom, blushing, 'but she has run away.'

'No compunction in your heart, Tom?' said the father, shaking hands with him. 'No remorse for robbing an old fellow of his only treasure, and leaving him lonely? Eh?'

'You set a bad example, sir, some thirty years ago,' said Tom. Lording exploded in one of his great ringing laughs, but there were tears in his eyes all the same which were not altogether born of laughter.

'She's a good girl, Tom,' he said, 'though I say it. A good girl. And if she's as good a wife as she is a daughter, you'll have a treasure. But one word, my lad. You mustn't run away with her yet awhile. I must have time to get used to it, and to think it over. Now, Tom, you've done your business—ride away, and tell your father. Yes; I turn you out of doors, like a wicked father in a novel. Go away, lad, and tell the old fellow to get ready to lose his son, whilst the other old fellow gets ready to lose his daughter. You'll see her to-morrow. She wants to see your friend painting, and I promise to bring her over. Good-afternoon, lad, and God bless you!'

Tom went unwillingly, but he went. Pleasant thoughts were his companions as he rode homewards. Arrived, he told his father of the prosperity of his suit, and submitted to a lengthy dissertation on the responsibilities of married life. After dinner he sat with Baretti in the room set apart as a temporary studio, and listened pleased to the little man's animated chatter. There was a fire at one end of the room, and the Italian stood rubbing his hands over it, cigar in mouth, and basking in the cheerful glow.

'This is better than St. James's Park, Carroll,' he said at last. Tom's outer ear caught this statement, but his mind was deaf to its meaning. He was thinking of Mary, and he answered mechanically—

'Yes. I suppose it is more comfortable.'

'Ah, my friend,' said Baretti, who was liable to be run away with whenever he mounted this theme, 'it was not that I was hungry, and had no food. It was not that I was cold, and had no fire. But it is terrible to despair, and I despaired when I met you. There is nothing I have in the world, there is nothing I ever shall have which I do not owe, and shall not owe to you.'

'Look here, Baretti,' said Tom; 'once for

all, I won't have it. It was a bargain between us that that time should be forgotten.'

'It shall be forgotten,' cried Baretti, fierily, 'when I grow to be a hound and a scoundrel. It shall be forgotten when I lie and rot in my dishonourable grave. But not an hour before. And I have no way to repay you. You want for nothing. There is nothing I can do for you.'

'Stupidest of men!' said Tom; 'you have repaid what I lent you, and there is an end of it.'

'What did you lend me?' cried the artist, flinging his cigar into the fire. 'A handful of dirty money which you did not want, and which was nothing to you because you did not want it? And what beside? Nothing but hope when I despaired; nothing but my belief in men, which I had lost; nothing but my power to work, which had left me! If I am happy, and can hope again, I owe it to you.

If I reach to fame and prosperity, as I shall, the fame and prosperity are yours by right, not mine. And you want for nothing, and I can pay you nothing.'

He declaimed every word of this harangue with vivid passion and superabundant gesture. There were tears in his dark eyes when he closed, and he fawned upon Tom almost as an affectionate dog might have done.

'What shall I do for you? How shall I pay you? If you shall come to me one day and say: "For my service surrender everything—Fame, Ambition, Hope, whatever is dearest to your heart," do you think I would not do it? You made me, and you own me.'

'All this is madness,' answered Tom. 'You don't know how it hurts me to hear you talk like that. Now, my dear good fellow, don't say any more.'

'I know,' said Baretti, with a curious darkness clouding his face as he spoke, 'but you may live to prove me.'

'Now, there you are on a wrong tack again,' said Tom. 'I don't doubt you. I only say that you exaggerate to the highest degree of absurdity a very simple service. If your own idiotic, Quixotic pride had not been in your way, a thousand men would have done as much for you.'

'Aha!' cried the little painter, with out-stretched hands, 'but where were the nine hundred and ninety-nine? It was you who did it, and you cannot escape from it; and I will be grateful, if you were to kill me for it. I have never,' he added, with a ludicrously sudden return to the tones of commonplace, 'I have never admired that stolidity of character on which you English pride yourselves. Ariosto's fable is true. God found one day a lump of gold, and he wrapt it in lead and cast it upon the earth, and that was the English people. And you have been ashamed of the gold, and proud to show the wretched lead ever since.' He was in a great heat of scorn by this time, and flung the moral of his fable at Tom's head as if it had been a challenge to mortal combat. But in another second he had veered to his old manner. 'Why cannot I do anything for you?'

'Well, look here, old man,' said Tom, with something like an inspiration, 'since I am such a burthen to your soul, you *shall* do something for me. Something I shall value so highly that even you, seeing how I prize it, shall admit that we are quits.'

'I do not think that,' said Baretti; 'but tell me what it is.' There was such a look upon him as Curtius, his countryman, might have worn when he leapt into the gulf.

'It's nothing mad-brained or heroical,' said Tom, with an embarrassed laugh. 'I want you to paint a portrait—that's all.'

'Yours?' demanded Baretti eagerly.

'No, not mine,' said Tom.

'Whose?'

The young fellow returned no direct answer to this question. He asked in turn: 'You don't know why I went out this afternoon?'

'No,' said Baretti, with a wondering look at him.

'I went out,' said Tom, making a pretence of lighting his cigar, 'for the express purpose of making—a proposal of marriage.'

'And you made it?' cried the painter, taking him by both arms.

'I made it,' said Tom.

'And the lady said " Yes," ' cried the little Italian. 'And it is her portrait that I am to paint. Thank you! Thank you! That is kind indeed!'

'Yes,' said Tom, thawing somewhat at his companion's fire. 'I want a portrait of the only woman I ever cared for, painted by the hand of the dearest friend I have in the world.'

'Ah!' said Baretti, vehemently. 'Do you mean that? Do you mean.that?'

'Yes,' said Tom, 'I mean it.' And in all real honesty he had long since begun to love the little man to whom he had done such a service.

'It shall be,' said the painter, with a beaming face, 'the dearest pleasure of my life, and I will paint as I have never painted before. I will paint like Murillo, like Raphael, like Titian—I will paint like the master of them all.' He went striding up and down the room, and then, suddenly pausing, seized Carroll by both hands. 'I am forgetting. My dear Carroll, with all my heart and soul I congratulate you. I wish you happiness and long life. Do I know the lady?'

'You have seen her,' said Tom, laughing

and blushing and shaking hands. 'You saw her yesterday, and I introduced you to her.'

Some new emotion knocked at the painter's heart, a sensation never felt before, swift and keen and painful. Carroll, in his pleasant embarrassment, was not looking at him, and the change in his face passed unnoticed. Baretti dragged his hands away from Tom's grasp and walked the length of the room.

'What men you are, you English!' he said, in a tone so curious that it struck the other strangely. 'You said she was a pretty girl.' He laughed, and Tom thought the laugh an odd one. 'A young man is in love. He is not a common young man, but an artist, and he has written music that makes me believe he has a soul. And one day, meeting the goddess of his dreams, he can turn to a friend who loves him, and say she is a pretty girl. You are beyond me. I give you up. I have no understanding for you.' Then he flashed back into his own fiery and enthusiastic tones. 'But I will paint her portrait—the beautiful English girl, in the freshness and the grace of her young womanhood, with the face of a kind angel and the figure of a queen. Ah! I will paint a picture.'

'I thought it would please you,' said Tom, simply.

'I congratulated you when I did not know,' said Baretti. 'Give me your hands again. Both hands. So. I know now, and I congratulate you again with all my heart and soul.'

Tom, laughing and blushing again, shook hands once more, and the theme dropped. The friends parted early, and the painter in his own room took out the work of the afternoon from his portmanteau, and after looking at it fixedly for a long time, set the edge of the paper to the light of his candle, and burned it slowly into ashes.

' Carroll,' he said softly, in his own tongue, ' there is no slave in the world who belongs to a master as I belong to you. You made me, and you own me. I am all yours, now, and till I die.'

CHAPTER VI.

Mr. CARROLL the elder was not a man to put any light he might have under a bushel, and finding out by-and-by that it was a creditable sort of thing (or was so esteemed by those who surrounded him) to have an artist of Baretti's capacity on his premises, he took to showing him a good deal. Mr. Carroll's world heard as much as enough of Mr. Carroll's portrait, and the painter sometimes worked with a little court of county admirers round him. He became extremely popular with the county ladies, and might have had his head turned if he had chosen to believe one-twentieth part of the flattering things they told him.

There are some spiritual maladies which

VOL. I.   K

can only be cured by being absolutely un-
meddled with and left out of thought. Grief
and hate and unauthorised love all belong to
this species, and a man or woman who tries
continually to discover how far the malady is
abated or increased is out of the way to a cure.
To examine the passion is to feed its egotistical
wish to be examined and thought about, and so
to nurse its growth. Every passion is in itself
supremely selfish and exigent, and there are
few that cannot be starved into subjection by
the mere coldness of neglect. Poor Baretti
awoke to the conclusion that he was near to
envying and hating his friend, and with all the
desire in the world to escape from that terrible
precipice of wickedness, he could not resist the
temptation to hover about it, to ask himself
how near he was—how much nearer he might
go without falling over; how much longer
he could stay at the edge before the heart-
vertigo he dreaded should prompt him to

throw himself headlong. To drop simile and get back to plain dealing, he examined himself continually to see whether or not he were in love with his friend's sweetheart, and found (as a natural consequence) answers within himself which became more and more dangerous to his peace.

Human nature is so hopelessly complex and contradictory that it is even possible that, but for Tom Carroll's attachment to Mary, and the painter's passionate desire to be faithful to his friend, Baretti might never have seriously fallen in love with her. He began to dread himself and to fear an admiration which, but for his fear of it, might have ended as a score of others had done before it. He did not begin to hate his friend, for so much wickedness could not find room in a heart so filled by simplicity and loyalty, but he did begin passionately to love his friend's affianced lover. The thing was always in his mind, and he began to be very unhappy, and to be so afraid of loving that by mere force of contemplation he loved. He was wounded to begin with, and under constantly inquisitorial fingers the scratch festered and grew mortal. At last, there is the truth of the whole matter, and conveyed in a simile, after all.

Baretti's portrait of his host was pronounced a fine work, alike by people who knew and people who did not know what they were talking about, and Mary Lording, who had seen the little man at work, and was more enthusiastic about his powers than anybody—being guided in that direction by her sweetheart's opinion, and going far beyond her leader, after woman's recognised fashion—was charmed at the idea of having her portrait painted by so gifted a personage. The painter himself, in the contemplation of the task before him, began to wade in dangerous waters, and in a little while got washed off his feet altogether and was abandoned to the tide, on which he sometimes drifted deliciously, but oftener deliriously, and oftener still in poignant misery of spirit.

On a lovely autumn day, bright and dry, and keen with the breath of approaching winter, the accepted lover and his friend set out together on foot in the direction of Lording's house. Baretti's painting tools had been sent on beforehand, but there had been some little uncertainty about the day on which the first sitting should be given, and it was not quite a sure thing that the lady would be ready to receive them. Arrived at the house, they learned that she was somewhere in the grounds, and Tom, being not merely an accepted lover but an *habitué* of the place since boyhood, went out in search of her, taking his friend with him. The grounds of Lording's mansion were varied and extensive, and what with laurel walks, rhododendron walks, and walks sunken from the surrounding level to secure shelter in winter and shade in summer, there was ample opportunity for a game at hide-and-seek. In the eagerness of the chase Tom took the lead, and he was twenty yards in front of Baretti and at the end of a fine avenue of beeches, when he turned, and smilingly beckoned the painter on. The latter quickened his pace, and was just in time to see the smile of recognition and welcome which lit up Mary's face at the sight of her lover.

On the left side of the avenue, approached by a meandering path between two great trees, lay a secluded little dell. This dell, being sheltered by the high foliage of the near trees, had kept for the most part a look of almost summer greenness, and the fiery hand of autumn had only kindled here and there a leaf. The moss which paved the place was a mere carpet of live emerald, and interlacing boughs above the lady's head made a sort of natural archway. This was the only hour of the day at this season at which the sun-rays could pierce the higher leafage, and the whole place was beautifully dappled with light and shadow. At the end of the vista revealed by the opening boughs lay a patch of richly-cultured garden, bright with colour; and nearer at hand, just where the arched foliage ended and the garden began, was a little fountain, whose one lithe and quivering jet sparkled in the sunlight, much as a gay melody sparkles on happy ears.

But the most charming feature of this charming spot was, of course, the girl who stood in it, smiling and radiant, like the day. Female loveliness is no doubt lovely in a cotton print, but when delicate fabrics of exquisite colour have gone through the hands of an artist who knows his business, in days when fashion gives him a chance to be graceful, they can give beauty an extra charm. The dress she wore was simple enough to look at, but it became her almost subtly. She had been gathering flowers and ferns, and carried them in a basket in her gauntleted hands.

There is no disputing in matters of taste, and there are no doubt thousands of men who, allowing the girl to have been beautiful, would have gone by without recognising their ideal. It was enough for Tom that she was his, and it was more than enough for Baretti that she was his also.

'Can you give us a sitting?' asked Tom gaily. 'Baretti is here and ready.'

'I am here without doubt,' said Baretti, 'but I am not ready.'

'No?' asked Tom, turning upon him; 'why not?'

'I want this,' said Baretti sombrely, 'to be a picture as well as a portrait. And I cannot begin at once as if I were painting a house. Can I paint here to-day, Miss Lording?' he asked, 'or shall I carry my things back to Trench House?'

'There is a room in complete readiness,' said Mary, with a half-puzzled look from Tom to the painter, ' but I thought you said that you did not want to begin to-day.'

'I do not want you to sit to-day,' said the painter brusquely. 'I want to sketch. I have an idea. Can I go?'

' Certainly,' said the girl. Tom possessed himself of the basket, and they walked to the house together. Baretti did not speak until he found himself in the room set apart for him.

' I want to be alone, if you please,' he said then, and began to push his easel about the room, and to raise and lower the blinds. 'I do not wish to be disturbed until I have done what is in my mind. It is now eleven o'clock, and I can work till half-past four. I shall have done by then.' He was very gloomy and quiet about all this, and Mary smiled at his exaggerated earnestness. Tom stayed a minute or two to chaff his friend, but, meeting with no response, he left the room and took away Mary with him.

Being alone, the painter shut and locked the door, and taking a small mounted canvas, set it on the easel, and began to work. For half an hour his face of gloom grew darker and darker, and then his changeful nature set him on a new tack, and he began to work smilingly. Then in a while he was gloomy once more, but he worked all the time like a man possessed by an idea. It was not long before the idea began to declare itself. By swift and sure degrees there grew upon the canvas the figure of a girl who stood in a little green-floored dell, embraced by surrounding boughs and bearing in her gloved hands a basket of tangled ferns and flowers. The distant garden began to smile in the sun, and the green flooring of the dell to dapple with light and shadow.

There was a knock at the door and Tom Carroll's voice was heard outside.

'May I come in?'

'No,' said the painter, without turning his head or pausing at his work.

'The bell has sounded for luncheon.'

'I am not hungry,' said Baretti; 'I shall not come to luncheon. Leave me alone.'

Tom retired, and the painter worked away. The face was merely indicated, and might have belonged to anybody or nobody, but the rest of the sketch had already something of a look of finish. Baretti lit a cigar and rested for a time, rising now and then to add a touch of colour here and there. When his cigar was smoked through, he cast the stump into the grate and went on again. Not a bristle touched the canvas without definite intent, and he worked with prodigious rapidity and certainty, but with no hurry. The tints grew true, the eyes and lips began to smile, there came into

the face beneath the magic kisses of the brush
the glance of recognition and welcome he had
seen four hours ago; the very figure looked as
though it were about to move and to step from
the canvas.

The artist looked at his watch, laid down
his tools, and lit another cigar, pacing up and
down the room as he smoked. Next, he sat
and stared at his work from under gloomy
brows, until he detected a fault somewhere and
rose to amend it, and finding something else
too lightly indicated, put in a masterly stroke
or two of finish, and by these means became
spurred into labour once again. The light was
already growing dangerous to paint by when
he finally laid down his palette and brushes
and rang the bell.

'Tell your mistress and Mr. Carroll that
I am ready,' he said to the servant who answered this summons. The man retired obe-
diently, and a minute or two later Mary and

her lover and papa Lording were heard laughing merrily together upon the stairs. Baretti stood back from his picture and stared at it solemnly, with his hands in the pockets of his velvet jacket and his head drooping slightly forward, and in that attitude they found him.

'Man of whims,' said Tom, 'what is it? Mary! Mr. Lording! Come here! Baretti, you are a worker of miracles!'

The three stood before the work in amazement and admiration. Its effects were necessarily broad, but there was no hint of coarseness in its handling, and the colours were like nature's own. A rival painter might have discounted admiration a little, but there was no rival painter there, and the trio broke into unmeasured praises. The painter, with his head still drooping forward and his hands in his jacket-pockets, accepted their enthusiasm with an air of almost melodramatic gloom. He was genuinely unhappy now—more self-distrustful than ever, with more reason. He declined Lording's invitation to dinner, and, in spite of pressure, went away alone to lock himself in his bedroom at Trench House, and brood over his own astonishing wickedness and the charms of his dearest friend's affianced wife.

'Baretti,' said Tom, as he sat at table with Mary and her father, 'is a man of genius, and, as everybody knows, men of genius have moods. I suppose he had worked everything out of himself in that splendid inspiration, and felt fit for nothing afterwards. Small wonder if he did.'

His companions took that view of the case also, and not even the girl, as yet, began to suspect the truth. But, meantime, the little man was exceedingly bitter with himself, and yet, for his soul, he could not resist the ever-returning vision of the girl's face and figure. Though he turned it out of mental doors a thousand times, it came back again, beautiful, smiling, unconscious. And he had vowed eternal faith and friendship to the man who had saved him, and who had an unassailable claim on all this loveliness. He tried to soothe himself by the casuistry natural to his position. He could love without wishing to possess, but his heart cried out in indignation against that folly. It went through him like a knife when he thought of her in Tom's arms, and fancied Tom's kisses on her lips. At least, he could love and be quiet; but again, at that thought, the future seemed to rise before him like a blank wall. And the more he chafed and argued, the more his fiery longing grew, till his southern blood, hot enough by nature, reached almost to boiling point, and he saw how dangerous he was growing. You may guess from what you know already that resolution was not his strong point. No resolute man would have gone-under as he did on such poor compulsion, and if there was anything to save him now it must be something outside himself.

'After all,' he said, ' to die of thirst in the desert whilst you watch your friend's only glass of water is a hard thing no doubt, but it is not stealing the water.'

He sought whatever safeguard he could think of. Amongst them was the difference between Miss Lording's position and his own. Love her as much as he chose, even if she had been free, she would not have looked at him. Then, in face of that reflection, he began to dream of fame and fortune, and he saw himself as a new Titian, the acknowledged king of art in his own day, living in a house like a palace, and surrounded by social courtiers. But of all possible safeguards he felt that there was none like his friendship, and, though his inward panegyrics on Tom Carroll were more forced and less natural than they had used to be, he had recourse to them and magnified Tom's service, and minified his own chances without that splendid friend and helper, until he began to experience a dawning sense of security. How could he be faithless to such a friend, even in fancy—even in a dream?

It was pretty late at night when Tom knocked at Baretti's door. The painter admitted him, and shook hands in silence. Tom was quite radiant and full of high spirits, and he must needs rally the small man of genius about his moods.

'What a droll fellow you are, Baretti! To-day, deeper sunk than plummet ever sounded; to-morrow soaring sky-high, and breaking your sublime head against the stars. But that's the penalty you pay for being a man of genius, and an Italian. Come into my den, my lion, and have a quiet smoke and a talk.'

'Very well,' said Baretti, with a more lowering face than ever; and having replenished his fire, and blown out the candles upon the mantelshelf, he followed. Tom's room was bright with firelight and lamplight, and its gay owner, talking voluble nothings, bustled about it, drawing curtains and pushing chairs near the fire. Talking still, he explored on his hands and knees the lower shelves of a locker, and arose with an aspect almost tragic.

'Not a spot of liquor in the ship!' he said. 'Wait a bit, whilst I go and look up Johnson. The governor's in bed, and I don't want to ring.'

Baretti nodded, and setting his arms on the mantelpiece, between the lamps that burned softly at either end, stared drearily at his own features in the mirror, without consciously seeing them. Tom Carroll was away so long that the little man forgot him.

'So,' he said to himself, 'this is the end of my pretences of gratitude.' It looked inexpressibly dark and ugly to him as he faced it in his own mind. 'No, no, no. They shall not end in this way.' As he moved with his Italian swiftness of gesture in answer to the movement of his soul, the motion was reflected in the mirror and drew his eye to the duplicate of his own figure there. He looked at it darkly for a minute, and shook a menacing finger at it. 'You!' he said fiercely and disdainfully. 'You!' The reflection shook back at him a finger as threatening and as disdainful as his own. 'I tell you,' he said, 'that you shall not moan about this, that you shall not admit to your own heart that it lives, that you shall carry it away and bury it, deep, deep, deep—do you hear?' The mockery of his features in the glass faced him and seemed to answer him. 'I shall have trouble with you,' he went on, apostrophising the reflection. 'You will mock me and storm back at me when I storm. You cannot be happy? You? Then it remains, my poor foolish friend, to be unhappy, and still to be a man. And you shall be as unhappy as you choose, but you shall not have one memory of a thought to curse you for having proved unfaithful.'

Tom's foot kicked gently at the door, and Baretti, answering to the summons, admitted his friend, who bore a bottle in either hand and one under each arm.

'Practising for the stage?' asked Tom, laughingly.

'No,' said Baretti, turning lightly round. 'But I never shall be rid of my Italian accent.'

'There is not much that is un-English in your accent,' answered Tom, setting down his bottles; 'but your action is altogether alien. You dart about like a parched pea in a pan. We English stand solid and lumpish while we speak. Now "speak a piece" as the Yankees say, and I will drill you. Something English.'

'Danish will do,' said the painter, with no responsive smile, and he declaimed with his arms hanging at his sides, and his whole figure stiffly set. 'Give me the man that is not passion's slave, and I will hold him in my heart of hearts—'

But here on a sudden he cast his arms wildly in the air and made a rush at the impassive Tom, crying—'as I do thee!'

'Something too much of this,' said Tom, completing the line, and shaking Baretti's hands away from his with a gesture that had nothing unfriendly in it. 'This is less English than ever. We must train you by duller methods. Let us try the prosiest of prose to begin with. Repeat me one of Euclid's axioms.'

'A straight line,' said Baretti, marking the straight line in the air with a rapid forefinger, 'is the shortest road between two points.' And out stretched both forefingers at the end of the imaginary line, to illustrate the position of the points.

'You are hopeless,' said Tom, laughing. 'A man who gesticulates over Euclid will gesticulate over anything—over everything. I wonder,' he added with sudden seriousness, ' whether you southern people feel as keenly as you seem to feel. It seems to an Englishman —you don't mind my saying this, Baretti, do you?—that the Italian manner indicates— indicates—what's the word? Not insincerity ? '

' No,' cried the painter, almost fiercely, ' not that.'

' No,' said Tom, holding out a hand to beseech quiet, ' not that, but a certain brevity of duration in sincerity. A flash and over. An intense appreciation of anything and everything whilst it lasts. Your passions, fancies, likings, rages, are all like lightning. You live by lightning, with the flash always coming and going.'

Baretti shook his head.

' There is steady fire enough in an Italian's heart,' he answered, with a sombre nod, ' to warm your hands at. I will give you another reason for the flashes you speak of. If you have a dull, steady, slow-burning fire, and you throw any trifle into it, any bit of stick or straw, you have a little flame which rises and dies. But you do not say that the fire is out, though it looks dull by contrast, when your wretched little bit of stick is finished. Human nature is human nature all the world over, only you show your emotions like an oyster, and I like a—like a——'

'Grasshopper,' suggested Tom.

'That will do,' said Baretti, with perfect gravity. 'He is a sunny little creature who loves warm weather, and he moves briskly and he sings, though his tunes are all very like one another.'

'And yours are not,' answered Tom, 'for you are Variety's Epitome.'

'There is no deep-rooted distrust of Italy in all this, is there, Carroll?' asked the painter, with a pretence of badinage. 'What am I? A butterfly little fellow, eh? Fluttering, hovering here, there, no staying, no resting, no stamina inside to make me want to rest and stay.'

'No, no,' said Tom; 'I don't read you so badly.'

'You do not think that I could not make my mind up to do a painful thing, which would take a long time, and be painful all the while?'

'No,' said Tom, lightly enough; 'why should I?'

'I do not want an answer of that sort,' said the artist, with a fiery sweep of his right arm. 'Do you believe of me that, for the sake of principle, or for the sake of a friend—for you, for instance—I would do something hard to do? That it is in me to do it? In a word, that I am a man of principle, and not an insect of impulse?'

'Granted,' cried Tom, in some surprise at his companion's heat. 'Granted every word.'

'You mean that?'

'I mean that.'

'From your soul?' demanded the Italian, vehemently.

'I believe it honestly,' answered the Briton, with genial stolidity.

'It will be better for me, and for you,' answered Baretti, 'that you do believe it.'

'I'm very glad to hear it,' said Tom, lightly. 'Whisky or Burgundy, old man?' Baretti cast at him a glance of rage and threw up his hands.

'Oh, you English! you English!' Tom laughed. Baretti was so much in earnest about trifles that Tom took nine-tenths of his talk with a cent. per cent. dilution. In his inmost heart he thought an Englishman the only solid and responsible creature in the world.

'Carroll,' said Baretti, ' I am uncomfortable. I am in want of something, and I think it is music. Play something to me.'

'All right,' said Tom. 'The governor's bedroom is on the other side of the house, luckily, and I shan't disturb him.' Tom took up his violin and began to play.

'Stop,' cried Baretti, two or three minutes later; 'I am out of tune. Your loveliest melodies caterwaul to me. I do not care for Mozart any more than if I were a Carib. Put it away, or play to yourself, if you will, and I will say good-night. Good-night, Carroll, good-night.' Tom tried to dissuade him from going, but he stood with both hands outstretched for a farewell, and a strange smile on his face. The player laid down his instrument and took both the outstretched hands in his, shook them, and dropped them gaily. The artist went without another word, and having locked the door of his own room and stirred the smouldering fire, he relit his candles, and, with his elbows spread abroad upon the mantelpiece, fell to staring at his own reflection. He had stood for a long time, when he murmured to himself:—

'Not one base word of Carthage on thy soul!' Then he suddenly blew out the candles, so that but for the glow of the fire the room was dark. 'Good-night,' he said softly, 'good-night, Carroll. Best man and dearest friend, good-night. It is not the dog you fed who will bite you. It is not the heart you gave its only hope to that will envy you.'

He sank into a chair beside the fire, and watched the glow until it faded and died. Grey ashes were sprinkled, slowly, slowly, on the heads of faces in the fire, and glowing features crumbled one by one until all had gone the way to dusty death, and he was staring blindly at the darkness.

CHAPTER VII.

NEXT morning, when Mr. Carroll and Tom and Baretti were at breakfast together, Master Tom, who had a considerable little pile of letters before him, opened one of them, and, suddenly rising from his seat, began to caper about the room and to sing and snap his fingers.

'Thomas,' said Mr. Carroll, with a voice of displeasure, ' pray compose yourself.'

'Read that,' said Tom, throwing the letter on the table and stooping to right his fallen chair. 'Isn't that magnificent?'

Mr. Carroll, with his gold-rimmed double eye-glasses on the bridge of his nose and his head thrown back a little, read the letter which had so delighted his son.

'This pleases you?' he asked, when he had gone through it. He held the glasses in one hand, and the note in the other, and tapped them together lightly as he spoke. 'This pleases you?'

'Certainly,' said Tom, whose face was already much less radiant; 'it is the greatest honour I could have hoped for.'

'M-m,' said Mr. Carroll, putting up the glasses once more, 'I should scarcely have construed it so. You will answer the—ah— the gentleman who writes this in the affirmative?'

'Why, my dear father,' said Tom, in a little dismay, 'I never was so proud in my life. It's a letter from Hoffmann, Baretti,' he went on, turning to his friend. 'They're going to play my "Dream of Venice" at Hoffmann's Wednesday Concerts, and Hoffmann wants to know if I will conduct in person.'

'It is a splendid opportunity,' said Baretti.

'It is a high honour. I congratulate you, Carroll, with my whole heart.'

Mr. Carroll drew out his snuff-box, tapped it twice or thrice, and put it back again.

'Very well, Tom,' he said, handing back the note again; 'I trust that I can rely upon you to do nothing which will endanger my respect. You belong to your world and I to mine, and I suppose we shall not convince each other.'

'There are to be two rehearsals,' said Tom, who was so checked in the full flow of his spirits by his father's manner that he was fain to hide his embarrassment by a pretended reperusal of the letter, 'and Hoffmann wants me to be present at them. The first is in a week's time. Shall you begin the portrait to-day, Baretti?'

'Yes,' said Baretti, 'to-day. You will come with me?' Tom assented, and the two finished breakfast in silence. Mr. Carroll betook himself to the library, carrying his letters with him, and before the two young fellows left the house they heard him ride away to attend some meeting of the justices in the neighbouring town.

'I'll tell you what it is, Baretti,' said Tom, ' my father's a sort of survival. He is a man of the old school, and he is slow to imbibe the modern feeling about art. You know how new that feeling is in England ?' He was obviously afraid lest Baretti should feel in his own person the lash of Mr. Carroll's scorn of the artistic classes. The little man nodded back at him, with a singular smile, wonderfully affectionate and gentle.

'Yes,' he replied, quietly, ' it is hard to surrender the opinions of a lifetime.' He spoke with so little of his common vivacity that Tom noticed it, even in the midst of the preoccupation of his own annoyance. They were in the lane together on the way to Beech

Tree Hall, and the artist was walking with his
eyes upon the ground.

'What is the matter, Baretti?' asked Tom,
with a hand on his friend's shoulder. 'You
are changed.'

'I will tell you the plain truth,' said the
artist, pausing in his walk. 'You must not
laugh at me,' he went on, looking upwards,
with a blush, 'but I am home-sick. It is three
years since I last saw my native Naples, and
then I stayed but for a week. There is nobody
left,' he continued, sadly, 'but the place is
there, and I must see it again and live in my
own air for a time.'

'That's natural enough,' said Tom. 'When
do you want to go?'

'I shall finish this portrait,' answered
Baretti, 'and then I shall go away at once.'

'You won't stay long?' Tom asked.

'I cannot tell,' replied Baretti, 'but I will
promise one thing. If you will let me know

when you are going to be married, I will come
back in time.'

' A bargain,' said Tom gaily.

' A bargain,' echoed the painter. 'Very
well.' A fortnight in the poisoned sunshine of
her presence and then blank darkness. In all
ages young men and young women have found
love's dream look thus real and thus lifelike.

Tom told his good news to his sweetheart
and her father, and found ready sympathy and
congratulation.

' But Tom, my lad,' said Lording, drawing
him on one side, ' what's going to become of
the portrait? You won't take Baretti with
you? When you are gone he'll be lonely.
Let him come over here. I'll ask two or three
people to come down and stay whilst he's here.
Eh ? '

This promised to be something of a relief
to Tom, who, now that he came to think of it,
saw clearly enough that Baretti would hardly

be comfortable if left to the sole society of Carroll senior. So the Fates arranged between them that Antonio Baretti should be proved. He had no excuse for declining, and his perturbation on being asked was taken to express no more than a little shyness. He was so afraid of the real cause of his unwillingness being guessed that he made next to no resistance, and before work was begun that morning the thing was settled. On the day before Tom's departure for London, Baretti was to take up his abode at Lording's house, and stay there until the portrait was finished. Then everybody was to go up together to witness Tom's triumph at the concert—for, of course, nobody thought success doubtful—and Baretti, after the concert, was to start for his native Naples.

Miss Lording had an easy time of it, and Baretti scarcely called upon her. He was not morose, as he had been on the previous day, but his manner was subdued and softened. Mary felt herself surrounded by a novel and pleasing atmosphere. The smell of Baretti's paints was an ingredient in it, but that was inevitable and easily endured, and it was surely nice to have awakened an artist's artistic enthusiasm, as she knew she had awakened those of the Italian, and to have her affianced lover there to pet or tease as she would—by signs so slight as not to be detectable by two of the quartet present. Lording was proud of his daughter and proud of Tom, and proud of Baretti, and was generally in high feather. For Baretti this morning there was a sort of luxury in resignation. He had complete faith in his renunciation of the night before. There was no more need for resolution, and he had simply to be passive and to let time drift him along as rapidly as might be until he could go away and begin to forget.

There was a piano in the room, and Tom

sat down to it now and again and played a snatch of music. Lording watched the work of painting with a childlike interest, and Mary moved about gaily in the long and frequent intervals of liberty the artist accorded her. Once or twice she came so near to Baretti in her innocent ignorance, and stood watching the work so close behind him, that although no portion of her dress so much as touched him, her nearness was like an embrace, under which every sense of his frame and every faculty of his mind seemed to swoon. When she posed for him, sometimes gravely and sometimes overbrimming with gaiety, and he met the stedfast unconscious look of her lovely eyes, or saw the laughter of a young and innocent nature there, and the gladness of a beautiful harmless vanity, he felt as if he were sinking into some lovely perfumed dream to die. And all the while he went on working with a singular consciousness of power over his materials and his theme. Niagara was three weeks off, and the passage along the Rapids was endurable. The position was not a new one.

The most admirable and becoming arrangements are made by consent of society at large for the prevention of unaccompanied meetings between young men and young women, notwithstanding which young men and young women continue to meet without the society of their elders, to plan marriages of which those elders would righteously disapprove, and generally to conduct themselves as their elders did before them, and would again if they were young again. But since her mother's death none of those arrangements had been in force in the case of Mary Lording, and she had known and enjoyed a freedom to which most girls of her age and station are strangers. It followed in her case—though naturally enough it might not follow in all cases—that she looked on young men with a sort of sense of brotherhood and camaraderie, that she was not in the least afraid of them or abashed before them. It was true enough that they made love sometimes, and that (except in one special case) had always been disagreeable. Now of course nobody would dare to make love to her, and freedom was made freer than ever by that reflection. She would have associated herself quite fearlessly with any nice young fellow of reasonable position and antecedents, who happened to come to her knowledge by any of the recognised roads, and in Baretti's case she was prepossessed in half a dozen different ways. He was her lover's dearest friend—he was a young man (in Tom's belief, and therefore in hers also) of the most transcendent genius—he was handsome and charming and a foreigner—and—he had given very signal proof of enthusiasm about her portrait. Now, if you and I believed that a great artist was enthusiastic in his desire to commemorate our charming faces and figures, we should naturally have a good opinion of that artist's discernment, and should feel friendly towards him.

A profound melancholy laid its hand upon the artist when he was not at work, and this helped to make him interesting. He took interest in nothing that did not concern his art, except by fits, when he broke into vivid momentary enthusiasm and flashed back again into gloom. He avoided all society when he was able, and though he strove to do it naturally and as if it were always the result of accident, the girl saw that he specially avoided her. This piqued her, and set her with a woman's love of conquest, to vanquish his shyness and his desire for loneliness. So there came to be added to the little man's torments a dreadful sweet fear which brought temptation in its train. He was not a vain man, over and above the common, but it came into his heart one day to ask if the girl were drifting towards him as he had drifted towards her. If that were so he felt himself doomed, and there was an awful throb of joy at the fear.

If his melancholy had been at all of the stagey sort, Mary would have been one of the first young women in the world to laugh at him. But it was so real, so obviously unaffected, and so little obtrusive, that it not only piqued her into a desire to overcome the shyness which sprang from it, but extorted some pity from her as well.

Had Tom Carroll guessed what he was leaving behind him he might have declined Herr Hoffmann's flattering offer. To leave the only woman who had ever breathed a word of love to him (for they had got so far by this time at odd moments), and the dearest friend in the world in her society, could scarcely seem unsafe to so generous and candid a nature. And, indeed, it does sometimes happen that a man's best friends do not betray him, and that a sweetheart is true. He went off with a light heart, and nine-tenths of his ambition seemed already realised in fancy. To live a mere country gentleman's life, with no interest outside that narrow sphere, had seemed ignoble to him from his boyhood, and this one chance seemed to open up to him the whole world of art ambition, and with the forerunning enthusiasm which belongs to ardent young men of talent he felt like a Gounod or a Verdi already.

The great Herr Hoffmann received him politely, for a wonder, and the rehearsals passed away without memorable incident. Cousin Mark called at 20 Montague Gardens, and made himself agreeable in his own way.

'I have found a new profession,' said Mark.

'It pays just as well as the old one. Nothing a-year, and pay your own expenses.'

'Profitable,' said Tom lounging in his own arm-chair at the fireside.

'Isn't it?' said Mark, with his own cheerful and amiable smile. 'I am teaching the charming Signora to talk English.'

'What charming Signora?' Tom demanded. The memory of Signor Malfi and his mate had long since left him. Mark recalled him to the circumstance of their chance encounter.

'I find it useful to know them,' said Mark, with his customary candour. 'A poor devil like me has to fish for profitable acquaintances. You were born with a golden spoon in your mouth, and I don't suppose you ever knew what it was to want a fiver in your life. By God! Tom, I believe that of all the hard-up men in London, I am king and captain.'

'Well,' said Tom, with a rather fatuous

good-nature, 'you know where to come to.'
Mark laughed.

'I shan't leave you till I've drained you
dry,' he said. 'I shall never pay you even if
I am able, for I am by nature an ungrateful
dog, and gratitude has always seemed to me,
to tell you the honest truth, the most absurd
and misguided of all human sentiments. But
if you will oblige me with a tenner——'

Tom laughed responsive, and obliged him
on the spot.

'If ever anybody asks you for a testimonial
to character,' said Tom, 'don't offer it yourself.
Send him to me.'

'My dear fellow,' returned Mark, still
smiling, 'that sort of thing pays. If you pro-
claim yourself virtuous nobody believes you.
Everybody knows that all men are liars and
nobody believes anybody. Now I tell the
truth about myself, and nobody believes *me*.'

'Now, you know, Mark,' said Tom, who was

amused by all this, 'that's not a pretty sentiment.'

'Don't come to me for pretty sentiments,' Mark answered. 'I am the only man I ever knew who wasn't either a liar or a fool. Now, you don't like to own it, but you know that ninety-nine parts in a hundred of all the talk about virtue and honour and public spirit is pure and unadulterated humbug. When you want to hear the truth about a man, go to his enemies. They'll tell you how degraded his motives are. If you want the truth about Gladstone read the high Tory journals. If you want the truth about Disraeli read the low Radical papers.'

'Somebody says,' Tom responded, 'that the only way to understand a man is to love him.'

'What a rule for a British jury with a knotty case of murder! No, no. The true rule of life is to think every man guilty until he proves himself innocent. Then you can admire his skilfulness of fence and distrust him all the more.'

At this Tom fairly broke into laughter, and Mark, with his hand stretched out towards his wine-glass and his cigar half-way from his lips, laughed back at him quite gaily.

'I've got what I want,' said Mark, emptying his glass and rising, 'and now I'll go. I have to give the charming Signora her English lesson this afternoon. Do you feel inclined for a walk?'

'Yes,' said Tom, and in a minute or two, well coated, the cousins were in the crisp, wintry open air.

Tom thought little enough of Mark's rhodomontade. It was Mark's habit to profess cynicism, and the easy-going youngster, his cousin, with his kindly thoughts about all people, and his amiable heart, would have found it difficult to believe that any man really cared to regulate his life by such a creed. But

such conscience as Mark had was soothed by
the candour of his own discourse, though he
admitted that even whilst he spoke the truth he
expected nobody to believe him.

It was not a very honest exposition of his
own character after all, but if, with the plain
truth staring them in the face, people refused
to believe in it, was that Mark's fault?

'I don't know,' said Mark, as they walked,
'whether I am or not a particularly brilliant
teacher, but if I am not I have an especially
brilliant pupil. You remember when we met
that woman? She didn't know a score of
English words, upon my honour, and now she
can understand a lot that's said to her, and she
chatters away in a surprising manner. Come
in with me and hear her. She's amusing.'

'No, thank you,' said Tom.

'You will, though,' answered Mark, 'and
I'll tell you why. Malfi has got all the tenor
music of Hoffmann's new opera. He's a slow,

poor sort of creature, and it takes him a month
to learn a tune. The charming Signora plays
with one finger—for he doesn't know a note,
and she's not much better—and they hammer
it out in that way between them. He has
learned half a dozen of the airs now, and sings
them decently. He'll be grateful if a swell
pianist like yourself will give him a turn, and
I'm sure you'll like the music.'

'I'll go for that,' said Tom, 'though I
wouldn't for the broken English.'

'The charming Signora,' pursued Mark,
'has learned English enough already, under my
tuition, to venture on taking English music
pupils.'

'And she plays with one finger?' said Tom.

'Oh, that's my playful way of putting it.
She's a bad enough pianiste, but not quite so bad
as that. I wrote an advertisement for her a
week ago, for pupils, and sent it to the *Times.*'

When they reached the house in which

Signor Malfi had apartments the piano was in full swing, and a powerful soprano voice was screaming a bravura. The powerful soprano left off in the middle, and the accompaniment reverting to the beginning, another voice took up the air.

' No, no, no, no, no !' the Signora's voice was heard crying. ' Like zis,' and the powerful voice began to scream again.

' Here's a pupil,' said Mark, ' the first fruits of the advertisement, no doubt.' The pupil began to sing again, and Tom held up a finger to ask for silence. There was a look of perplexity on his face. ' What's the matter ? ' asked his cousin.

' That's odd,' said Tom. ' I'll bet anything I know that voice.' They were within the house, and waiting for the operatic tenor in the next room to that in which the lesson was being given. ' I'm sure of the voice,' said Tom, ' I can't be mistaken.'

'Whose is it?' Mark demanded, but at that instant the Signor entered.

'We are indebted to you, Signor Carroll,' said he to Mark. 'The advertisement has already secured a pupil, an English miss. It was a good thought, and it will occupy Caterina in my absence. I have engagements in Paris and Vienna, but she has not, and will remain here. There is a voice!' The screaming soprano was turned on again. 'For volume and compass it is unrivalled in Europe. Yet the managers will not engage her.'

The singer was disposed to be voluble on this matter, and he talked until Tom (knowing nothing of the language in which the conversation was conducted) strolled to the window, and, staring out on the street, fell into a day-dream. He was startled from it by the sudden slamming of the street-door, and a second later he saw a familiar figure — the figure of a girl whose skirts were blowing picturesquely in the wind, and who bore a roll of music in her hand.

'Look here, Mark,' he cried. 'Isn't that little Azubah Moore? You know! The little girl at the farm at home? We used to play with her when we were lads together.'

'By Jove, it is!' cried Mark, as the girl turned for a moment to face the wind and rearrange her dress.

'That is Caterina's pupil,' said the Italian, making an easy shot at the purport of their talk. 'She will never sing. She has not the volume or the compass.'

'What does he say?' asked Tom, and Mark translated. 'That's a matter of opinion,' said Tom, nodding his head sagely, 'and all the same, I'd sooner hear her than that railway whistle in the next room. What on earth made a singer marry a woman with a voice like that?'

'Marry?' cried Mark, smilingly. 'He's no

more married than I am. Buono giorno,
Signora Malfi,' said Mark, as the lady entered,
and he advanced to meet her with outstretched
hands.

CHAPTER VIII.

THE time of Baretti's stay was coming to an end, and the portrait was all but finished. Tom was back in the country and was over every day to look at the growing beauties of the picture, not being unmindful in the meantime of the charms of the picture's original. If there might have been found in all broad England a happy man, that man was Tom Carroll. As he rode or walked between his father's house and Lording's on those bright mornings and bracing nights, his heart welled over with joy, and he carolled in the lonely lanes like a throstle. A good heart, a good digestion, lots of money, ambitions opening, a sweetheart beautiful and kind, and the

dearest friend man ever had in the world
—what more might he desire ?

And all the while love and friendship
were fighting in Baretti's heart, and making
wild work of it there. The little man was
sensitive of honour, and all his intensest
desires and the secret hopes he tried to ignore were dishonourable.

Mary knew of his approaching departure
from England, and sometimes spoke of it,
not knowing the pain she gave him. Baretti
was at work on the last Monday morning
of his stay, and he was touching and re-
touching the ripened beauties of his picture
with a lingering hand and a heart disposed
to linger. From the canvas, the work of
his own hands smiled upon him with how
perfect a beauty ! What is old Fairfax's
verse ?

> Her hand, her foot, her vesture's hem,
> Muse, touch not for polluting them
> All that is hers is clear, pure, holy.

His brush kissed her shoe upon the canvas as his lips would have felt it too bold to do in fact. The best worship he could offer her seemed to soil her, for not only his love but his friendship made her sacred. A double passion made her doubly inaccessible, even to his thoughts, and yet his thoughts were rebels to his will and would assail her. And she sat there the while, chatting and smiling, stooping to the friendliest intimacy, and holding him miles and miles away.

'Mr. Carroll tells me,' she said, 'that you have no friends left in Naples.'

'None,' he answered.

'And yet you suffer from home-sickness? Do you love the place so much?' He shook his head and answered without looking at her.

'I have a double reason for going. But the reason I have given is light beside the reason I have not given.' She did not answer to this enigma, but looked at him with inquiring interest. 'A duty calls me there. I can say nothing of it, except that it is a duty, and a hard one. But in this world one does not always what is pleasant. Fate brings you nasty mixtures and does not care for your wry faces.'

'No,' she said assentingly. His sadness and his resignation touched her, and her tone was caught from his.

'There is a friend of mine,' he went on, mixing a delicate tint upon his palette, and keeping his glance resolutely fixed upon it, 'who did me a great service. I made a promise to him in return. He does not know of it yet, but I know that it is a thing of life and death to him that I should keep my promise now. I lose nothing by it, but there are circumstances which make it hard to keep.'

He had thought when he began that he could trust himself to say so much and no more, but a sudden terror fell upon him lest he should betray his secret. He stopped abruptly, and began to paint almost blind-fold. There was silence for a minute or two, and then he discovered that his work was going wrong, and busied himself in restoring it.

'I must not pry into your secrets, Mr. Baretti,' she said, after this pause, 'but it is easy to see that you do not like the task you are taking upon yourself. Are you quite sure that duty calls you to it?'

'My way is plain,' he answered. In an Englishman his manner might have looked a little over-dramatic here, but it was so evidently real in him that it passed for pure nature, as it was. 'I am bound by every tie of honour and friendship.' He began to feel a glow of strength and hope even as he spoke. 'And if I were what a man should be, I should not even feel a regret at doing it. When I am in my right mind I shall be glad that I have done it. It will be very disagreeable to do, and I am like a child who is offered medicine. That is all.'

'Your friend does not know yet that he needs your services?' she asked. If Mary Lording had only known it, she herself was going on a dangerous road. Her accepted lover, whom she had known all her life, and for whom she had a most sincere and tender friendship, had never interested her as Baretti did. But she had no time just now to stop and analyse.

'He will not know,' said the painter, turning his face upon her. She read a look of exaltation there which it was impossible for any man to have feigned. The flashing eyes and handsome face were transfigured by that emotion of friendship and the strength of soul by which he repelled temptation. 'He would only know that he had needed me and that I had broken faith if I did not keep my word. And he is a friend so true, with a heart so honest and kind, that when I think that I have been afraid to be a little uncomfortable when I do my duty, I am ashamed—ashamed.'

She had never seen him in such a mood before. Whatever the duty he had set himself might be, it was plain enough that it entailed more than a little discomfort, and his single-heartedness roused her to a momentary flush of enthusiasm.

'We shall all be sorry to lose you, Mr. Baretti,' she said, 'but not one of your friends will ask you to linger when you have such an errand.' And she held out her hand like a queen. Baretti dropped his brush, accepted the proffered hand, and bowed above it. She shook hands frankly like a man, and returned to her seat. Baretti picked up the fallen brush, and went on working, but she saw suddenly that he was as pale as death, and somehow, whether by instinct or by chance, she read his fable through and through, not as if by a guess, but as if by the light of absolute certainty.

She was conscious enough of her beauty, and was little to be blamed upon that score, for, apart from the innocent vanity which leads young people to think well of their own attractions, she had had hers so dinned into her ears by lovers who languished and lovers who stormed and lovers who wrote verses, and needy fortune-hunters who wanted money and had no objection to taking a pretty wife with a fortune, that she had more than the ordinary excuses for a knowledge of her charms. But she was a girl with a healthy mind, and a heart that had room in it for much more than the joy of being admired. Her first conscious mental act was to repel the fancy, but the fancy proved, sudden as it was, a fixed belief, and would not be repelled. Then a pang of pity and sorrow touched her heart, and then—was she sorry? For whom? For Tom—for Baretti—for herself? For a moment she felt as a swimmer feels when he floats unsuspectingly into a sudden, powerful eddy, and finds himself rolled helplessly over and over.

She had never doubted her affection for Tom Carroll, the steady growth of years of intimacy and pleasant intercourse. It was not the love she had read of in plays and books, and she had set down plays and books in her own mind as exaggerative if not false. That she could love a man whom she had not known for more than two months was palpably preposterous and unnatural. That she could be false to her dear old friend and newly-affianced lover even in a thought was a thing too absurd to need to be refuted. Each of these mental postulates stood unshakable, and yet—she sat in sudden terror of herself. If the man loved her—— ? She dared not face the result of that inquiry.

Baretti, with only self-possession enough left to know that he must still disguise himself, turned away from the picture, and began to scrape the colour from his palette. Mary arose, and, trying to speak naturally, asked :—

'You can do without me for the present, Mr. Baretti?' Her voice sounded strangely unsympathetic and cold, alike on her own ears and on his.

'Thank you—yes,' he answered hoarsely ; and not daring to commit herself to more words she withdrew. 'I have betrayed myself,' said Baretti, miserably. And then such a new foolish battle began within him as you may picture to yourself by the aid either of imagination or experience. First, he rejoiced to think that at least she knew he worshipped her, and then he was ashamed of his rejoicing. Then, at least, his sufferings were known, and then new shame rushed at him for that base hope. But at last, and after no very prolonged spell at

this old and unprofitable exercise, he resolved :
'I will finish the picture and go, and in the
meantime I will keep out of her way.' So he
hardened his heart, and in spite of his pitiable
state, he set to work again. Storms of noble
shame and ignoble joy swept through him, and
there were moments when he could neither
think of his work nor see it, but he held on
resolutely in the main. There was so little to
do that but for his love for the theme and his
loyalty to his friend he could well have borne
to leave it undone, and two or three hours of
resolute labour saw him to the close. The
luncheon-bell rang, and he disregarded it.
Lording came up in person to look after him.

'Too busy to come downstairs, Baretti?'

'I shall have finished in half an hour,' he
answered; 'I cannot leave it now.' Lording,
who had quite a superstitious reverence for his
guest's genius and its various urgencies, went
out on tiptoe, and excused Baretti to his guests

He had to excuse his daughter also, for she sent word that she was troubled by a headache, and kept her room till dinner-time, though Tom came over in the afternoon with only an hour to spare, and rode away disappointed. He drove over again in the evening, and found her languid and unlike herself, but he was better pleased that evening, in spite of the lover-like fears that assailed him, than he had ever been before in her society ; for she seemed to cling to him, and was so sweet and kind, and withal seemed for once so dependent on him that he went home in a state of blissful worship and security. It was natural, but more than a little pitiful. The poor girl wanted to make up to him for a second's infidelity, not daring to guess that the whole course of her life had changed, and the poor lad went away flattered and enraptured until he scarce felt mortal, and had no faintest notion that he had seen the last flicker of love's little flame. In two hearts friendship and honour struggled against a passion that has vanquished both a million times. But though love had conquered one, the other had not yet capitulated, and even in Baretti's case honour and friendship were pilot and steersman, though passion commanded the craft. And between them they played their captain false right staunchly, and the little man went his way sore but resolute.

Baretti's unfortunate parable had been set forth on a Monday; the concert at which Tom's work was to be played was one of a Wednesday's series; and on Tuesday from the two houses of Carroll and Lording there was an exodus. Thomas Carroll the elder, much as he objected to Tom's appearance, was not insensible to the flattering notice taken of the event by the local county people, and notably by my Lord Bellamy, who was an enthusiastic musical amateur, and he had consented to go up to London and listen to the performance. Lording and Mary were also going, though the girl now began to feel exceedingly guilty and un-happy.

'My dear,' said the old fellow, addressing his daughter an hour or two before the time fixed for departure, 'I want you to do me a favour.'

She asked him somewhat uninterestedly what it might be, and he, with a face of mystery, drew from his waistcoat pocket a tiny morocco case no bigger than a pill-box. This being opened revealed a ring with a splendid diamond set in it.

'This is for Signor Baretti,' said Lording, with a sly laugh. 'He painted that picture for Tom, you know, and of course we can't let a thing like that go unrecognised. Heaven only knows what it's worth! I'm sure I don't. A thousand pounds, perhaps. Now, I want you to give him this ring from me, and to ask him to wear it as a memento of his visit and his kindness.'

VOL. I. o

'Papa,' said the girl, with a look of wounded indignation, ' how can you ask me to do such a thing?   No, dear ; no.'

'Bless my soul!' cried the old gentleman, ' where's the impropriety? Never mind. There, there.   Never mind.   I'll give it him myself. Will you come with me?'

She assented lingeringly, and Lording, too dull of perception to notice her manner, led the way to the room Baretti had used as a studio. The artist was putting up his brushes, and after the manner of lovers, was making inward protestations above the senseless things that had been associated with his passion. He would keep them till he died, and they should never touch canvas any more, having once been glorified by such a theme. But, indeed, as some of us remember well enough, the slightest things grow sacred to a lover.

'Signor Baretti,' said Lording, in his bluff, hearty way, ' I've something here which I want you to be good enough to accept as a little memorial of your visit here. I hope you'll wear this for my sake, and that you'll think of us sometimes when you look at it. It's not much of a gift compared with the beautiful work you're leaving behind you, but it's just a little souvenir of my daughter and myself, and we shall both be very pleased if you'll accept it.'

The painter looked and felt embarrassed. Compared with his host he was a very poor man indeed, and the gift looked like a payment.

'Pray take it, Mr. Baretti,' said Mary.

'I am very sensible of your kindness,' said Baretti. 'I will never part with it.' He was so obviously affected, though Lording had no guess as to the real reason of his discomposure, that the old gentleman himself found it necessary to blow his nose, being, as he was, exceedingly susceptible to all sorts of friendly emotion.

'Nice-hearted little fellow he is, to be sure,' he said to his daughter a minute or two later. 'Takes to people like a dog, doesn't he?'

It was scarcely the commendation Mary would have chosen had she been in a mood to commend him, but she said nothing, and went away to superintend her maid's preparations for the journey.

When the journey came it was a dull one. Mr. Carroll had a pompous disapproval of its object, and smiled superior above the age which permitted a gentleman to play such tricks with his position. Baretti and Mary were silent, and Tom was crushed by his father. The talk devolving chiefly on Lording, that excellent old fellow kept things going for awhile, and at last went to sleep over his *Times.* The painter left them at the London terminus, and went to his chambers, taking his belongings with him, hoping to breathe freely once again and knowing his hope futile. The quartet went to an hotel, and awaited the event which had brought them all to town.

In spite of the energetic applause of Lording and Baretti the 'Dream of Venice' achieved but a qualified success, and fell a little flat upon the audience. On the morning after the performance Mr. Carroll scanned the critiques in the daily papers, and was confirmed in his opinion that the pursuit of artistic honours was unworthy of a gentleman. Nobody had ever dared to make quite so free with the name of Carroll as these anonymous and irresponsible reviewers. None of them were warm and some were frigid. 'If this young composer,' said the Censor, 'desires to prosper in his profession, and to secure the public ear, he must,' &c., &c.

'Thomas,' said Mr. Carroll, with a pitying smile, 'read this, and tell me if a pursuit in which your position is so liable to be misunderstood is a pursuit to be adopted by my son?'

Now Tom, although he was as good-natured

a young fellow and as submissive to paternal
authority as need be, was a little sore
that morning about several things. To begin
with, faint applause is as bad as downright
damnation to an ardent seeker of the arts, and
Tom had seen himself in fancy on the way to
Fame's pinnacle when the great Hoffmann
condescended to produce his work. The disappointment was hard to bear. He had tasted
the last of his sweetheart's sweetness, for the
girl was beginning to be sore distraught in her
own mind, and seemed almost apathetic about
the whole matter, deeply as it concerned him.
Baretti had his own troubles to think about, and
sincere as his friendship was, and genuine his
belief in Tom's genius, his praise had sounded
forced and unreal. And so in his soreness
Tom answered his father disrespectfully for
the first time in this history or out of it.

'Position!' cried Tom. 'Good heavens,
sir, what is *my* position?' Mr. Carroll sighed

and smiled, with pitying eyebrows raised again.

'It has been the object of my life,' said Mr. Carroll, neither in sorrow nor in anger, but with a resigned allowance for his son's aberrations, 'it has been the object of my life to instil into you a proper understanding of that position. The age is tending downwards, Tom, and I am not so wanting in perspicuity that I cannot see it, or that I cannot allow for the effect it has upon your conduct. But I am not eager to see my son foremost in the race for degradation.'

'Degradation!' cried Tom hotly.

'Degradation was the word I used,' said Mr. Carroll, with unusual severity of manner. 'I will thank you not to echo my observations in a tone which I can only characterise as dishonouring to yourself and me.'

'Will you kindly tell me what I have done, sir?' asked Tom. There was a little of the old man's obstinacy and vanity in him, though his better qualities obscured them.

'My dear Tom,' said his father, waving his large white hands expressively. 'My dear Tom.' He went with great deliberation through his usual snuff-box pantomime, and even got so far as to raise the lid. He closed it with a snap and restored it to his waistcoat-pocket. 'Think the thing over, Tom,' he said, with the nod of a man who is prepared to give another a chance. 'I am not without faith in your natural good-sense, and it is possible that last night's fiasco may have taught you something.'

'Fiasco!' said Tom.

'I repeat the word,' said his father. 'When a gentleman stoops to such a proceeding as yours of yesterday, nothing can atone for it but the outstripping of all competitors.'

'Forgive me, sir,' returned Tom, 'if I close a discussion conducted in such terms.' He left the room in a great heat, and that was the beginning of a quarrel between father and son which left a certain estrangement, even when the outer breach was healed.

The youngster was flinging out of the hotel when he met Baretti.

'I have come to say good-bye to your father and to Mr. Lording,' said the artist. Tom turned back with him and led the way to Lording's private sitting-room. Mary was sitting with her father, and bade Baretti a collected good-bye, and her manner, remembering how close they had been together for the last month and more, was more cool than courteous. The ordeal was a severe one for Baretti, but he had schooled himself to go with it, and he gave no sign which anybody but the girl could read. Mr. Carroll that evening returned to Trench House, and Lording and Mary also left London. Nobody felt in very high spirits, and even Lording was dashed by Tom's succès d'estime.

It was evening when the disappointed musician returned to his own chambers in Montague Gardens. He sat moodily by the fire for an hour, and heard Baretti packing overhead. By-and-by, remembering how sad and woebegone the little man seemed at leaving England, in spite of his home-sickness, Tom's good heart began to warm again. He would go and cheer his friend a little. His slippered feet made no noise upon the stair, and Baretti's door was ajar. He pushed it wide, and entering, stood amazed and solicitous. The painter, in his velvet sacque and his gay slippers, was kneeling at a great arm-chair with his head buried in the cushion, and his whole frame was shaking with sobs, though he gave scarcely a sound. Tom backed out, gently drew the door to its old position, and went silently downstairs.

'He has some trouble of which I know nothing,' said Tom to himself. And as the thought crossed him, the painter rose from his knees in the room above. He had been kneeling over Mary Lording's picture, the first sketch for the portrait, and the beautiful face glimmered uncertainly through the tears which had fallen from his eyes upon it. There are more ways of being strong than one, and Baretti's was the weak way. The weak, unwise, little fellow kissed the picture and locked it away in one of his portmanteaus. He was never cut out for a hero, and it was hard to run away from the delight of her presence. But if he were not true to Tom Carroll, friendship was a farce, and there was no such thing as honour in the world.

CHAPTER IX.

'Tom,' said Mark, comfortably lolling in Tom's most comfortable arm-chair, and smoking one of Tom's cigars, 'why don't you learn Italian? It has always been a wonder to me that you never went in for it.'

'I ought to know it,' said Tom. 'Everybody who goes for music ought to know Italian.'

'Then why not learn it?' asked Mark.

'Oh, I don't know,' said Tom, with a disgusted look. 'Such a lot of trouble.'

'Nonsense,' said Mark, 'a mere distraction. I'll tell you how to do it pleasantly. Come and sit at the Signora's lessons. You'll help her English and she your Italian.'

'Well, I don't altogether care,' Tom answered, after a little pause, 'I don't altogether care about mixing with people of that sort. Unmarried ladies who reside with married men who live apart from their wives are not much in my line.'

'Pooh!' said Mark. 'My dear Tom, the maxims you cherish would have served admirably for your grandmother to work on samplers. There never were any wicked ages and there never were any moral ages in spite of all the lies historians tell. There have been ages when what is called Vice—which would do very well for Virtue if it changed its name—has been hidden, ages in which it has been published, and ages in which it has been condoned. This is an age in which it is condoned. Pardon me, my dear Tom,' continued Mark, with his own characteristic smile, 'if I seem to assume a clerical tone with you. You are very young for your years, Tom. Your heart is fresh and in-

genuous, and your memory is faithful to the
traditions of the past. You remember your
copy-book morals. And what the deuce, my
dear fellow,' cried Mark, rising to his feet, and
taking his cousin by the shoulders, ' what the
deuce have we to play at age for! Crabbed
age and youth cannot live together. Shake off
dull care and come with me. A young eye
beneath a grey eyebrow is a prettier thing than
a grey head on young shoulders. And, all
nonsense apart, old fellow, you'll do me a good
turn. I am the sort of man who, all nonsense
apart, generally wants somebody to do him a
good turn.'

' How?' said Tom. You had only to put
it to this foolish young fellow that you needed
a good turn and he was at your service
instanter.

' Well,' returned Mark, ' I'm not vainer
than my neighbours. It's no tribute to good
looks, for ugly men have as good fortune as

handsome men, and sometimes better. It's no
tribute to my wit, for the dear creatures absolutely prefer to fall in love with fools. It says
nothing for my moral character. I'm not
proud about it. It's a confounded nuisance in
point of fact, and I'm simply unable to help it.
The Signora, Tom, has taken it into her Italian
head to fall in love with her English master,
and I'm a little bit afraid of her. I thought
you might like to learn Italian, and I thought
that while you did so I might secure a little
immunity from danger. You see, I can't give
up the lessons very well until I have fulfilled
my promise. It doesn't matter. If I get an
Italian dagger between my ribs, you'll see me
decently buried, won't you?'

'I don't mind coming,' said Tom, 'though
the idea of having *you* to chaperon is a little
droll, isn't it? When are you going next?'

'This afternoon,' returned Mark, 'if you
can come. But not otherwise, for a thousand

pounds. She has wonderful eyes, Tom, and when she plants her elbow on the table and drops her chin into the palm of her hand and languishes at me for half a minute at a time in the middle of the verb " To Love," it's a little dangerous. Confess it ? '

' I don't know,' said Tom. The Signora's bold black eyes had no charm for Tom. There was only one woman in the world for him.

' You would know,' said Mark, laughing, ' if you tried it.'

' I'm not so sure of that, either,' Tom responded. ' I don't think I'm very susceptible to that sort of thing.'

' I am,' said Mark, laughing again. ' But you'll come, won't you ? '

' Oh, I'll come,' said Tom. ' But where's the Signor all this time? Why doesn't he look after the lady ? '

' Well, he's a curious fellow,' answered

Mark. 'He's not jealous on the surface. He goes about and takes his own liberty a good deal and leaves her to take hers. But if he had a thought that things were going wrong, he's the sort of man to be on the spot with bowl and dagger in a minute. I'm glad you've promised to come, though there are only ten lessons more on the programme. By that time you'll have warmed to the work, and I'll go on with you at any times you like to mention until you've finished. It's a pretty tongue.

> " I like the language—that soft bastard Latin,
> That melts like kisses from a female mouth." '

And Mark began to spout Italian verses. Tom listened, tranquilly amused.

'You pretend to be a cynic, Mark,' he said ; 'and yet you're crammed with innocent enthusiasms.'

'Am I not?' cried Mark, with his own smile. 'What a complex creature the human animal is, isn't he, Tom? Come, we'll lunch somewhere together and then drop down stream to the Signora's.'

Tom was not altogether at his ease, but after all, the thing was a trifle, and Mark was very right in the main. Nobody seemed to think so much of one's associates now as they had used to do. The idea of having Mark to take care of tickled him a good deal, and he was pretty sure that some companionship seemed necessary or Mark would not have asked for it.

'If I were a humbug,' said Mark, after luncheon, 'I should draw out my purse and make a lingering pretence of paying the bill. I should then discover that I had left my last five-pound note at home. Not being a humbug I confess my poverty. How devilish nice it must be to have money always! Were you ever in want of a sovereign, Tom?'

'Many a time when I was at school,' said Tom; 'but not since.'

'Lucky dog!' cried Mark. 'Pay up, old man, and we'll make a start. I won't smoke restaurant cigars whilst you have one of those Principales in your case. Thanks.'

The two cousins strolled calmly in the bright winter afternoon to the residence of Signor Malfi, and there went through the Italian-English lesson. The whole affair was severely business-like until the end, and the Signora made no eyes at Mark. But when they were preparing to go the lady suddenly addressed Mark in her own tongue.

'Your companion,' she said, suavely, 'will not understand one word of what I am saying?'

'Not a word,' responded Mark. 'You may be quite sure of that, if you speak rapidly.'

'Then why did you bring him here?' she demanded. 'The poor, slow, stupid innocent!'

'Will you allow me to explain another time?' asked Mark. 'I have very good reasons.'

'You will be there to-night?' said the Signora.

'Without fail,' Mark answered. 'You have been angry all the afternoon without cause. But I like you best when you are angry. Anger becomes you. There is nothing that does not become you, and you make darkness fair.'

'You are a mocker,' cried the lady, gaily. 'Go now, but do not bring the stupid innocent any more. Good-bye.' She turned to Tom and addressed him in her liquid, pretty, broken English. 'It is pleasure to see you here, sir. I hope you will come often with Mistare Carroll.'

Tom shook hands and protested he was very happy, with little more sincerity than the Signora herself displayed.

'What had she to say to you in Italian?' he asked, when they were clear of the house.

'Well, to tell the truth,' said Mark, turning a smiling face upon him, 'she asked me not to bring you again, presumably because you interfered with her love-making. But you won't desert an old chum on that account, will you?'

'Oh,' said Tom, disgustedly, 'cut the lessons altogether. Bother the woman, with her painted eyes and her painted eyebrows and her confounded patchouli!'

'My dear Tom,' returned Mark, taking his cousin's arm and speaking in a serious tone, 'you know me well. You know that I make no pretence to be a moral fellow, and that I'm not given to atone for sins I am inclined to by damning those I have no mind to. Very well. I have made a faithful promise here, and in return for that promise—which was made before I saw any danger in it—have received certain favours. Small things, all of them—boxes at the theatres and that sort of thing—but something to a poor man like me. I have accepted these and I have made a promise. Now, I'm not a particular fellow, but I *must* keep a promise. Leave me a rag of virtue, Tom!'

'You are welcome to all you have,' Tom answered, lightly, ' but get the thing over as soon as you can, and then drop it. I wish you'd find some other victim than myself.'

'See me through it, Tom,' said Mark, almost appealingly; 'your virtue in this instance is its own reward. She is really a very cultivated woman, though I cannot guess how she and Malfi came together, and she has a beautiful accent. And it's thoroughly worth your while to learn.'

Tom assented, much against his will. His objections to the charming Signora were unforced and genuine. The lad was in love, and Love taught him to nurse a lofty ideal of all feminine worth. He thought of Mary Lording's innocent though imperious beauty,

and he unconsciously set beside her this flaring,
painted Southern woman—a tea-rose beside an
overblown holly-hock.   And Tom was one
of those young men—rarer nowadays than
they should be—who find in purity a woman's
crowning charm, and see in Virtue a something
so sweet and majestic that it brings them almost
to their knees.

With him, to think of Mary was pretty
generally to think of his own unworthiness of
so much grace and goodness, and now that
his failure had humbled him without overmuch
dispiriting him, to think of his unworthiness
was immediately to resolve on being worthy.
There seemed at such times only one way of
deserving her.   She sat side by side with his
art, and if he could but once climb so high as
to clasp the knees of his Goddess of Music,
he were high enough to touch the hem of his
sweetheart's vestal garment also.   In such a
mood he went home and locked himself in for

study.   Midnight found him slaving away at
a chorus of revellers for the opening of the
second act of his opera, and he was on fire
with his theme and could hear the voices peal-
ing, and the trumpets snarling, and the noise
of fiddle and flute and hautboy and the rest,
all dashing onward in one sparkling cataract
of sound.

Cousin Mark that evening grilled a chop
in his own chambers, opened a small bottle
of claret, and took his frugal dinner alone.
Then he made a cup of coffee, lit a cigar, and
surrendered himself awhile to pleasant medi-
tation.   The cigar being finished, he cleared
away, placing the soiled table utensils in readiness for the morning laundress, and having
banked up the fire, assumed his hat and coat.
He was standing in the hall with his finger on
the key of the gaslight there, when a faint
tap sounded at the outer door.   He stepped
forward on tiptoe and made a reconnoissance

through an almost imperceptible slit cunningly cut through the door at the deepest sinking of the panel. There were duns in the world, as Mark (being not merely a poor man but averse to parting with money when he had it) knew to the cost of comfort. This was a late hour for a common business dun, but there were plenty of people whom he would rather avoid meeting than meet.

The stairs and the landing were but dimly lighted, and he could not make out much of his visitor until, after tapping a second time, the figure retired a little to look up at the gaslit fanlight above his door. Then he knew it; and opening the door, stood hat in hand before the Signora.

'Caterina!' he said, raising his eyebrows with a singular smile. 'This is indiscreet, is it not?'

'It matters little,' she answered, 'whether I am discreet or not. Let me in, Marco.'

'Certainly,' he said, 'if you wish it. But remember I have never asked this of you.'

'I know it,' she answered, as she passed him. 'I am cold. You have a fire, have you not?'

'There is a fire in the sitting-room,' he said, closing the outer door and waving her along the hall. She entered the room and he followed.

'Marco,' she said, reproachfully, 'I had expected a little warmer welcome.'

'My love,' he answered, 'I am so surprised to see you here! What shall I do to show how glad I am to see you? Pray sit down whilst I stir the fire. We shall have a fine blaze presently. Now, let me take off your cloak.'

'No,' she said, coldly, 'I can help myself.' She escaped from his too solicitous attention, and removing her hat, stood to arrange her hair before the mantelpiece mirror. Then with a single motion she slipped from her cloak and threw it over a chair.

There are more ideals than one in the world, and in spite of Tom Carroll's cordial distaste for her, the Signora was undoubtedly a fine woman in her way. A subdued light was favourable to her, and the gaslight was low. The fire began to flicker a little, and to light up her cheek, and her ripe lips and bright eyes, and to lay sudden flashes of gold-colour on the lights of the coal-black hair. Mark was something of a connoisseur in female charms, as has been said already, and he thought the Signora had never looked to so much advantage since he had known her. He was too much of an artist in his own way to desire to spoil the colouring of the picture.

'Do you find this half-light pleasant?' he asked. 'Pray sit down. I think nothing more charming than firelight.'

'Yes,' she answered, 'I have heard of that

as one of your English tastes. But, Marco, do not let us talk of trivialities. I am in need of sympathy. I am unhappy, Marco, unhappy, most unhappy.'

'Tell me your sorrows,' said Mark, in his softest voice. He really spoke Italian amazingly well for an Englishman, and his voice was round and musical. She was still unseated, and he approached her.

'Can I trust you?' she asked. 'Say nothing. I have had experience enough of vows, and I know what they mean. Let me look at you. Let me see your face whilst I speak to you.'

She moved suddenly, and turned the gas to its full height.

'A moment, my dearest,' said Mark, turning the lights down a little. 'I am a poor man, and cannot afford to crack even a gas-globe wantonly. Now I am ready for inspection. Do you think I look honest?'

His voice had something of reproach in it and his face was serious, though he bubbled with mirth beneath his mask of earnestness. 'If you knew how much better you look in a more subdued light, my dear,' he said to himself, ' you might spare your face an ordeal. You don't need to rouge, but Tom was right, and the eyes and eyebrows *are* a little assisted by art.' He wore a tender and appealing look whilst he thought thus, and stood with his hands reaching a little forward, as if to say, ' Look your fill. There is nothing but honesty here.'

' Marco,' she said, ' you look honest : and you have sworn over and over again that you love me.'

' Love you ! ' he answered ; ' I worship the ground you tread upon ! '

' Odd,' said the real Mark Carroll, laughing under his mask. ' They don't believe it, and yet they like to be told so. Human nature loves to be humbugged.'

'I think,' she said, 'I *think* I can believe you.'

'Believe me?' cried Mark, 'I am simple honesty itself!'

'An Israelite indeed,' added the inward Mark, 'in whom there is no guile.'

'Tito's jealousy and harshness grow beyond control and beyond endurance. But I have no friends and no money, and I am in a foreign land, and you know what lies before me if I leave him. Can I trust you to be kind and good to me always? No, Marco, no! I shall be plain and middle-aged very soon, and then I shall have no charm for you.'

Mark turned abruptly to hide the smile which would crease his lips and sparkle in his eyes in spite of all his efforts. He carried off the effect of that abrupt avoidance of her glance by pacing with an angry-looking jerk in his step once up and down the room.

'There is no faith in a woman's heart,'

he said, when again he stood before her.
' None.'

' Marco,' said the Signora, plaintively, ' I
would willingly have faith in something.
I would willingly believe that love is not
altogether a vision, a dream, a mockery.'

Now the amazing part of the business
was that this Italian young person (who had
seen a good deal of the very worst side of the
world, and had learned to be wise, and had
been taught over and over again the folly of
staking gold against counters) was absolutely
in earnest. It was all good fun to Mark, of
course. If a pretty woman chose to throw
herself at Mark's head he was not the man
to say her nay. The dear creatures had
strange ways, and above all things in the
world they loved to be humbugged. Well;
he had no objection to giving them their own
way so long as it cost nothing but a little
play-acting.

'Caterina,' he said, 'if I were a wealthy man—if I could offer you a home befitting your own divine charms—would you scrutinise my motives in this way? But because I am poor you doubt me.'

'Will you let me share your poverty, Marco?' she asked, passionately. 'I could be good with you. I could be at peace again. I would be true to you. I would work for you. I do not want fine clothes. I do not want fine rooms. I can do without all those things. I only want a little love, Marco, a little kindness, a little peace. And since I have known what love is, Tito is hateful to me.'

She swept her gloved hand across her eyes, and Mark stole an arm about her waist. Up to now the Signora had furnished very good sport to Mark, but here the game had turned to bay, and he himself seemed likely to be hunted.

'Mia carissima,' said Mark, tenderly, 'you

know I love you. A passion like mine is not to be doubted. No woman ever lived who would not recognise a tenderness so devoted. You know it. Your own heart tells you that I love you. But you propose a thing impossible —at least for the present. Let us meet when we may. Let us extract what moments of sweetness from the bitter hours we can.'

'You love me,' she cried, ' and yet you bid me go back to Tito! No, no, Marco. That is not the love I want. I want peace, Marco— peace and rest—the peace and rest you promised me. Not that.'

'We must wait for that,' said Mark, sooth- ingly. 'I am so poor, Caterina, that I can scarcely provide for myself, and if I accepted the generous offer of your foolish heart we should both starve together.'

'If I go back to Tito,' she flashed at him, suddenly, 'I stay with him for ever. I hate him, and my life is all a lie with him, but I will not live a double lie. Oh, I hate all the world—myself—and you, because I love you so.'

'Let her have her head,' said Mark, with inward quiet, though he feigned to be perturbed and pretended to soothe her. 'She'll race herself out of breath in a little while. We've had thunder and lightning enough,' he went on, with a change of simile, 'here comes the rain. In half an hour we shall have clear skies again.'

If it had been possible to sit down in shelter, and to smoke whilst the tempest raged, Mark felt that the situation would have been passable. But it was a decided nuisance to have to make love to a crying woman whose eyes were actually growing smeary whilst she wept.

'She doesn't guess what a face she's making,' said Mark. 'But I shall at least have the advantage of seeing her au naturel

when the paint is all gone. It can't last long
at this rate.' And all the while he was sooth-
ing her and patting her hand, and making
the most chivalrous love in the world.

'No, Marco,' she said at length, 'you do
not love me. You do not care to be alone
with me.'

'Caterina!' said Mark, upbraidingly.

'No,' she said, 'you do not, or why should
you have brought that stupid innocent this
afternoon. If it had not been for him I
should not have been angry, and then I
should not have quarrelled with Tito, and then
I should not have come here to scold and cry.
Why did you bring him?'

'Caterina,' said Mark, 'listen to me and
be reasonable. Tito is growing jealous, and
I brought my cousin as a blind. I am not
very much of a coward, but if Signor Malfi
is to be hanged at all I prefer that he should
be hanged for killing somebody else.'

q 2

'Do you think Tito guesses that you love me?' she asked.

'I know it,' he answered, scarcely able to suppress a smile. The swarthy Signor's jealousy was a little more urgent than Mark's affection. Mark knew that, and he had a keen sense of humour.

'Marco,' cried the Signora, 'he is dangerous.'

As the words left her lips there came a loud knocking at the door, and she sprang to her feet with a suppressed scream.

'Be quiet,' said Mark, calmly. He kicked off his shoes and crept out to reconnoitre, and when he came back he was a trifle pale. 'Tito!' he said in a whisper, and the Signora looked about her like one in deadly terror. 'You are safe enough,' said Mark, seizing her by the shoulders and shaking her pretty sharply to bring her to herself. 'Come this way. Step lightly. Take off your shoes. Now take them in your hand. This way.' He himself seized her hat and cloak, and stepping like a ghost, led the way into the hall. The main door opened upon a double set of chambers, one of which was empty and unlet. Mark, who liked to know things, had found that one of his keys fitted the lock, and being as cool as a cucumber in this somewhat awkward strait (directly the first shock was over), he called this fact to mind and utilised it. There was another loud knocking at the outer door as Mark stooped to apply his key. He took advantage of the noise to move quickly, and thrusting the Signora into the cold darkness of the next hall, he closed the door, whipped back into his own room on tiptoe, pulled on his slippers, threw off his overcoat, hastily disordered his hair before the mirror, and walked out to meet his visitor.

He opened the door, and casting both arms in the air, yawned portentously.

'Is that you, Malfi?' he asked in a sleepy voice. 'Ugh! How cold it is. Come in. I am glad to see you. One gets diabolically dull of an evening sitting all alone, and I must have fallen asleep. I heard a knocking and dreamed that I was at the siege of Sevastopol.'

CHAPTER X.

THE swarthy fat man looked hard at Mark and listened to his speech without reply. His breathing was thick and heavy, though Mark had given him ample time to recover from any bodily distress the mounting of the stairs may have caused him. The barrister cast his arms abroad afresh and yawned as if he would fall in pieces, and the singer still stared hard at him without a word.

'Come in,' said Mark, with admirable calmness. 'Don't stand there in the cold.'

Signor Malfi without a word walked in and Mark closed the door behind him.

'Is there anything the matter?' asked Mark, appearing suddenly to notice the sin-

gular pallor which lay on the singer's dark
skin, and the remarkable expression of his
eyes. Malfi looked round the room deliberately and his stertorous breathing sounded
noisily distinct in the silence of the place.
' Why man,' cried Mark, ' you look as if you
had seen a ghost.'

Signor Malfi surveyed him darkly for a
moment, and still without a word took up a
candlestick which stood upon the mantel-shelf,
and set it upon the table. Mark saw that his
hand shook slightly as he drew a case of vestas
from his pocket, and striking one of the
matches, held its flame to the wick of the
candle. As a matter of course Mark knew
what was going to happen, but he was not
such a fool as not to be downright amazed by
the Italian's proceedings.

' My dear Malfi,' said Mark, in well-acted
wonder and commiseration, ' what is the
matter? What can I do for you? '

Signor Malfi threw the vesta into the fire, took up the candlestick, and walked into the hall, Mark following. The singer having examined the fastenings of the door, shot the two bolts, which had almost rusted into the sockets with long disuse.

'Are you mad?' said Mark, seizing him by the shoulder. 'Speak. Tell me what is the matter, and what you want?'

'I shall find what I want,' said Signor Malfi, opening his lips for the first time, and nodding at the barrister with a wicked look.

The Signora heard the shriek of the rusty bolts, heard Mark's questions and Malfi's answer, and scarcely dared to breathe as she listened, crouching behind the door.

'Come, now,' said Mark, with the air of a man who is beginning to find it hard to keep his temper. '*What* do you want? If my opinion is worth anything you want a strait-waistcoat.'

'Come with me,' said Malfi, looking at him with half-closed eyes. 'I will show you what I want.'

He walked back along the hall, and stooping at the sitting-room door found a key in the lock. He closed the door and turned the key, and then, light in hand, made for the little kitchen where the laundress left her work undone as a matter of daily routine.

'You madman!' cried Mark. 'Stand still.' He swung the Italian round and looked at him with searching inquiry. 'Tell me what you want,' he said, slowly and deliberately, as if to carry understanding to a mind not easily apprehensive of ideas. 'Tell me what you want, or I shall have to call for the police and see you taken care of. You must know that you are not acting like a man who is in possession of his faculties. Now,' gently and coaxingly, 'what do you want?'

'Bah!' said Malfi, with a sudden flash of light in his sickly, half-closed eyes. 'Do not play with me. Let me go. Oh, yes, yes, yes, yes, yes! Your eyes are made to look honest enough, but I can see the lie behind them. Let me go.'

'What do you want?' asked Mark. 'What do you mean by walking into my apartments in this way? Tell me. I will endure no more of this folly.'

'My good friend,' returned Signor Malfi, with a very singular smile, 'you will endure me until I have made my search and have found what I want. When that is done I will go, but not before.'

Mark cast his hands abroad in a sort of resigned desperation.

'Very well,' he said. 'You must have your way, I suppose. What do you want to look for? Where do you expect to find it? Go on and have done with it. Mad!' said

Mark in an inward-sounding voice. Mad! quite mad!'

'You are a very good actor,' said Signor Malfi, nodding at him. Something of the look of certainty the Italian's face had hitherto worn faded from it as Mark returned his gaze. With nearly all men the assumption of a facial expression begets an answering inward emotion. The genuine pretender is more easily affected in this way than another, and Mark had now so long been looking amazement at his visitor that he almost began to feel it. He only waved his hands in answer as if to say that this obvious madman must be borne with and humoured for a moment.

Malfi pushed by him with a look of renewed decision, and Mark followed, interrupting him no more, but standing resignedly by. The Italian's search was complete enough, but it led to nothing. He prowled over the whole place, candlestick in hand, and the owner of the chambers, having lit a cigarette by this time, followed him with an aspect of resigned boredom, as of one who had given up wonder.

'Now will you tell me what you wanted?' he asked.

'Where have you hidden her?' demanded Malfi, with an ugly coolness.

'Oh,' said Mark, 'there is a lady in the case! My good sir, I am not so honoured or so blest as to have a lady in these poor rooms of mine just now. Pray complete your search if you are still unconvinced. Take your time, and do not allow me to stand at all in your way.'

So saying he sat down in the arm-chair, threw himself comfortably back into it and crossed his legs.

'Where have you hidden her?' asked Malfi again, with the same threatening quietude of manner.

, 'My good friend,' said Mark. 'My rooms are perfectly open to you, and you may look through them until you are satisfied. As a mere affair of detail, I should like to know of whom you are in search. Do I know the lady?'

'This once,' said Malfi, 'you have baffled me. But you have not changed my mind, and what I knew before I came here I know still. I shall go now——'

'Thank you, sir,' said Mark, sweetly.

'But before I go I will tell you that I am not a man to be played with. If I killed you here in England they would hang me, and I do not want to be hanged. You will do me a favour, therefore, if you will keep out of my way.'

'You do yourself less than justice,' answered Mark, with his sinister smile. Easily as he seemed to take it all, he watched the Italian as a cat a mouse, and stretching out a lazy hand to a little drawer in his writing desk, he drew out a toy revolver. 'Signor Malfi,' he said playing with the pistol as he spoke, 'I should be a fool if I pretended not to understand you clearly. I should not be a man of honour if I treated you simply with the contempt your conduct deserves, and left you to the misery of your own mad fancies. It is likely enough that you will not believe me, but I declare—not for your sake but for hers—that I am innocent of any design against your domestic peace—that I esteem your wife too highly to approach her with any other sentiments than those of respect and friendship.'

'Yes,' said Malfi. 'It is not difficult to lie.' He moved towards the door, speaking loudly. 'And if she is within reach of my voice, as I believe she is, she will know, as you know, that I am a dangerous man to cross.

'You are an amusing vagabond,' said Mark

lightly, as he rose to follow him. 'Good-night.
If I am troubled by you in future I shall apply
to the police—not for protection—but for
delivery from a nuisance. On the other hand,
Signor, you may rely upon me to trouble your
domestic bliss no further. May I ask you
to draw back the bolts? Thank you. Good-
night. Allow me to turn up the gas a little.
You may find the stairs dark, and I would not
willingly disappoint your friend the hangman.
Good-night.'

To all this Signor Malfi answered not
one word, and Mark, closing the door behind
him, set his eye to the narrow crevice at
the top of the lower panel and watched his
burly figure as he went downstairs. Then,
after a little pause, he drew out his keys,
and stealthily and silently unlocked the door
of the next set of rooms. The Signor, Mark
reflected, might still be listening. He was
out of sight and hearing after the first turn

in the stone staircase, and Mark was dis-posed to be wary after what had happened.

Caterina slipped towards him out of the darkness like a ghost. She was pallid with cold as well as fear, and when she opened her lips to speak, Mark laid a finger on his own and motioned her in silence to the sitting-room.

'He is gone?' she asked in a terror-stricken whisper as she crouched above the fire.

'He is gone,' Mark answered, slipping back the toy revolver into its drawer and seating himself calmly.

'Marco,' she said, 'he is dangerous. What shall I do? How dare I return to him? He knows that I am here.'

'He thinks so,' said Mark tranquilly, lighting a new cigarette at the fire of the old one.

'Marco,' said the Signora, turning on her

knees before him, 'you are very cold to me.' Mark shrugged his shoulders and smoked. 'Give me a kind word, Marco, after all this danger for your sake.'

'My dear child,' said Mark quietly, 'love-making is a very pretty pastime, without doubt. But in this case I scarcely care for it. I was never of a romantic turn of mind, and as I grow older I grow more matter of fact. I care more for peace and a quiet mind than I used to do.'

The Signora, still kneeling before him, glanced at his face keenly with a miserably hungry look growing upon her own. This cynical and heartless young man had some-how reached to what heart she had. After all, it does come to most people at one time or another to pin a heart to somebody, to set soul and faith and purpose all on some one creature. And sooner or later, except to the very happiest (and the truest) the

golden dream grows grey, and faith is seen
misplaced — your kohinoors and emeralds
of Candahar are profitless pebbles and
beads of glass, and you break your
heart or turn stupid according to your
nature. Take the world round and it is
probable enough that love is a vice of the
blood, and a permission of the will much
oftener than the romancist cares to fancy.
And yet love reigns, and is king of all
the passions still, and will be till the whole
world's summers have deceased.

It was never profitable to tell some sort
of stories, which are now happily, by growth
of civilisation, taste, and heart, grown quite
unprintable in England. It would serve
no purpose worth serving to tell the story
of the Signora Caterina Malfi here. It had
been in the main an evil story, though, as
it affected her until now, not by any means
a sad one, and all through most unwomanly

womanly. Probably, until she met Mark Carroll she had never known that she had a heart at all, and he was but a poor god before whom to throw it when she found it. But you must allow sincerity of worship in the blindest idolater. Have there been no raptures of uplifted spirits before the ugly and foolish gods of India, and Egypt, and Great Britain ?

A pure life is much for a man. For a woman it is almost everything. It would be but a poor service to Caterina and her like if her historian should paint her as having a love as worthy to bestow as another woman might offer. And yet it was all she had, and the first she had known of goodness and purity. Everything is comparative, and in this case the purity of womanly passion was all the more amazing by contrast with previous old experiences.

‘ Is love-making no more than a pastime,

Marco ?' she asked. She had been terribly frightened, but a great fear will fly before a greater. Nothing the swarthy Signor could do could hurt her like a doubt of Mark. Mark shrugged his shoulders and went on smoking. 'Is love no more than a pastime, Marco,' she asked again, ' with you and me ?'

'My child,' said he, placidly dispelling a little cloud of smoke by a wave of his hand, ' the play is played out. We will close the box and put up the puppets. You don't know Thackeray, do you ?' he asked in English, with an attempt at a smile.

' The play is played out ?' .she asked. ' Marco, you do not mean you do not love me ? That we——'

' Love,' said Mark, ' is a charming word, and in its way a charming thing. But it has a tender and delicate life, and often dies early. In plain Italian, my good Caterina,

I am not going to run the chance of finding an Italian dagger in my ribs to oblige any lady, however charming she may be.'

'Well,' she said, with wonderful quiet, 'tell me everything. Say all you have to say.'

'There's a sensible girl,' said Mark. 'We go our ways, my dear, that's all: you yours, I mine. As for love, I have loved a time or two before this, and shall love again. And so I fancy have you, and so will you again.'

He expected tears and protestations, in accordance with the history of old days. He had seen that sort of thing before, and disliked it excessively because it bored him. But Caterina only rose to her feet and confronted him silently.

'You have some little toilette to make,' said Mark, pointing to the boots and hat and mantle, which all lay together in a disorderly heap upon the carpet. 'Whilst you make it I will see if the coast is clear. I am not altogether certain but that our mutual friend is waiting round the corner with a carving-knife in readiness for both of us.'

She said not a word, and he pulled on his shoes and overcoat, took his hat and gloves from the table, and with a word to say that he would return in a moment, left her. She heard the door close, and listened to his step until it grew inaudible, but she never moved until he came back again.

'He has resigned the chase, Caterina,' said he as he re-entered. 'I am afraid he will be unamiable when you meet, but you have had experience of him long ago, and you will know how to manage him. Not ready yet? Do not allow me to disturb you. I am in no haste.'

'You mean all this?' she asked slowly and quietly. 'You can cast me off like this? You could swear for a month or two that you love me, and could take all I had left to give, and then throw me away because you are afraid to hold me?'

'I thought I had explained it all quite clearly,' said Mark.

'You could look so like truth,' she said, 'and yet be such a liar.'

'My good Caterina,' he answered, 'you and I, who know the world, are wise enough by this time, and experienced enough to understand each other.'

'You swore,' she said, 'that you loved me.'

'And you that you loved me,' said Mark. 'And we agreed to believe each other.'

'And you never loved me?'

'My dear,' he cried, 'you are a very charming and accomplished woman. Even without beauty your understanding would make you irresistible. Even without wit your beauty would conquer anything with a heart inside it. I recognised your intellect and I did homage to your beauty. I do both still. But I am something of a philosopher, Caterina, and I am apt to weigh the value of a thing to me before I pay a price for it.'

'And love is not worth the price? You are afraid of Tito?'

'I am not afraid of anybody,' he answered with the same calm and flippant tone. 'But I am not a fool. At least,' he added with a laugh, 'I am not fool enough to pay so much for——'

'So little?' she asked, filling up the pause.

'Precisely,' he responded. 'Although for gallantry's sake I searched for a prettier phrase.'

'You mean,' she said, 'that I am and have been no more to you than any other woman you may find? That I have been a month's toy to you, and nothing more?'

'My child,' said Mark a little fretfully, 'I don't want to say a lot of things that are unconventional, and—true; unless you force me. We have played out our play very pleasantly, and I am heartily sorry that the curtain falls so soon. But I—you know—I am a battered old man of the world, as young as I look, and you have had experiences. Let us do justice to ourselves and to each other. Let us recognise the hand of the inevitable, and part in peace.'

'Marco,' she said, 'it will be bitter to have to hate you?'

'Then why try to do it?' he asked. 'I don't hate you because I have to part from you, and you have as good a reason for leaving me as I have for leaving you.'

'And I have loved you!' she said, with such a bitterness and intensity in her quiet tones that he began to be half afraid of her, and to think her made of some other metal than he had fancied. 'You! I have lived all these years in the world without loving any-body, and I must needs love you at the end of it all. Ah, well, Marco! I am going now,

and you may think that you have done with
me. You thought Tito dangerous, you poor
coward, because a woman said so. You will
find me more dangerous than Tito.'

Mark laughed softly and took another
cigarette. Passion does not always show itself
in romantic ways, and the Signora sat calmly
down and drew on her discarded boots,
arranged her hair before the glass, tied on
her hat, and adjusted her mantle and her
gloves, all in the most business-like quietude.

'I thought I had found a man at last,'
she said then, facing round upon him, 'and
I gave him all the heart I had to give. I
would have loved you like a dog. I would
have let you beat me and starve me for a word
of love a year.'

'My dear,' said Mark, 'you prepare the
way for your antithesis most eloquently. You
are going to say that you hate me now, as well
as you ever loved me, are you not?'

'I am going to say,' she cried, 'that I will repay you.'

'For what?' asked Mark. 'You have really cost me very little.'

'I will repay you,' she said again. 'I will repay you. And now let me go, if you please. I cannot kill you here, but I will bide my time.'

'I am reprieved for awhile, then,' Mark answered, leading the way to the door. 'Good-bye, Caterina. I am really very sorry to have to say it, but when you come to think, you will see how much wiser it is for both. Good-bye.'

'You!' she cried, flashing suddenly upon him with a vivid and terrible passion in her face and voice. 'You! To have thrown a heart away on you!'

'An error, Caterina!' Mark answered, 'a fatal error.'

'Yes,' she said, with sudden quiet, 'a fatal error. Let me pass. Good-night.'

He stood awhile to watch her as she went

slowly down the stairs. She was undeniably a fine woman, and he was sorry enough to lose her.

'Like most of those southern women,' he said; 'she has a bit of the tiger in her. I wonder, Mark, if your unworthy person excited any real passion in her—there is such a thing unless all men and books do lie, and most of them do—or whether she wanted a little bit of play-acting at the finish. I hope at least,' he concluded with a laugh, 'that she won't carry melodrama into action. I shall be out of the frying-pan into the fire indeed if I have a pair of daggers waiting for me instead of one.'

This prospect so tickled him that whilst he washed his hands and face and dressed for the streets, he chuckled half a dozen times about it. The Signora with a resolute step marched westward in the meantime, and the Signor, standing in the shadow of Temple Bar, saw her emerge from the Temple archway, and followed in her footsteps.

CHAPTER XI.

IT is not easy to believe that there were many better men in the world than Mr. Anthony Bethesda. It is certain that there were few indeed whose outer man bore so plain a sign of inward virtue. He had a large and well-formed body, plump but not corpulent; a large and well-formed head, and large and well-formed features. He was not in holy orders, but he looked as though no other line of life were appropriate to him, and he wore black clothes of the usual low-church-clerical or dissenting-ministerial cut. His white tie was large and spotless. His fat hands caressed one another, and his face was an index to his heart. It was rarely to be seen without a smile upon it—a smile humble and benevolent—a smile which said distinctly 'God forgive me,' and in the self-same curve of lip and eyelid, 'The Lord bless *you*, my Christian brother.'

This good man worshipped at a large, square-built chapel in the south of London, and was by all accounted a shining light and a model of the Christian virtues.

Taking his walks abroad one London autumn morning, Mr. Bethesda saw in the near neighbourhood of his favourite chapel a big van discharging furniture at the door of a little house. A florid, grey-haired man of country aspect was superintending the unloading, and a middle-aged woman of decent middle-class exterior was assisting a very pretty girl in the porterage of light articles from the big van to the little house. Mr. Bethesda paused a moment to look on with an aspect of benevolent interest. No man need search his mind for apologies on the ground that he finds it pleasant to look at youth and beauty, and Mr. Bethesda was a widower and old enough to be the girl's father. At that hour of the day this outlying London street was very quiet. From half-past seven to half-past eight in the morning it was always lively enough, except on Sundays, and brisk enough again from six to seven in the evening, for at those times the tide of clerks and shopmen ebbed and flowed. At other hours the policeman, the baker, the coster-monger, the postman, and the muffin-man came alone to break the stillness of a desert solitude.

Apart from those who were personally concerned with the big van, Mr. Bethesda was the only creature in the street, and he was therefore noticeable. The pretty girl, with her hair escaping somewhat from its confining net, a flush of clear colour on her face, and a pleased excitement in her eyes, was emerging from the doorway, when she caught the good man's smile. Her face clouded curiously, and turning abruptly, she withdrew into the house. Mr. Bethesda lingered for a moment longer. He had more than a fatherly eye for a nice-looking girl, had Mr. Bethesda, and perhaps the young woman might return. Whilst he stood there the two men in charge of the van lugged to the mouth of it, with infinite trouble, a great old-fashioned wardrobe of black oak, and attempted to lower it to the ground. The weight was too much for them, and they called for help. The grey, florid man emerged from the house and lent a pair of hands.

'It is a Christian duty to help a neighbour,' said Mr. Bethesda, advancing.

'So I have heard,' replied the florid man drily, with an odd, distrustful sideway look at him.

'Allow me,' said the good man, either not observing or disregarding the other's manner.

Nobody objected to his assistance, and he lifted as strongly as the rest. The pretty girl was visible at the end of the passage, and it was evident that she took a keen interest in this proceeding. It is curious to notice how little will interest people who have not seen much of the world.

The ponderous old oak wardrobe was a fair weight even for four men to carry, and Mr. Bethesda was red in the face as he tottered at his own corner. Suddenly there was a trip, a stagger, and a cry. The grey-haired, florid man was down upon his back on the stone pavement; the man who had shared the load at that end was on his knees, and the weight had fallen with a sickening crash upon the prostrate figure.

'Father!' shrieked the girl, running forward. The man made no response. They moved the weight from his body and bore him indoors, but not before that part of the street was crowded with people who had suddenly sprung from nowhere. Mr. Bethesda entered with the two men of the van, but he seemed as helpless as the rest, and could do nothing but gape and stare with fatuous 'Dear me's!' Somebody ran for a doctor, and brought him elbowing his way through the crowd. A policeman, sprung from nowhere like the rest, stationed himself at the door and kept off intruders.

'Ladies,' said the doctor to the distracted girl and no less distracted mother, 'I must ask you to retire for the moment. You can be of use, perhaps,' turning to Mr. Bethesda. 'Officer, close that door, and drive those fools away. Now.'

The women waited in the hall outside the closed door, wringing their hands or holding to each other, and the minutes crawled like hours. When at last the doctor confronted them he was grave and had little to say. The injured man was still unconscious. It would be best to take him to the hospital. He would

receive completer attention there than else-
where.

Both the wife and daughter fought against
this and would hear nothing of it. What could
be done was done, and Mrs. Moore and her
daughter Azubah sat down to watch the
mainstay of the house, to see if haply he could
ever be so patched again as to prop their
humble roof-tree any more.

This was Michael Moore's London home-
coming, and to be brief about a mournful
business, the outcome of it was that the
hale farmer was crippled for life, and Mr.
Anthony Bethesda became the household
guide, philosopher, and friend.

The farmer mended slowly, and his wife
and daughter had deceptive hopes of him, but
he never got further towards health and
strength than to sit in a Bath-chair to be
wheeled about the streets on sunny afternoons.
Now sickness, more than any other form of

domestic extravagance, makes inroads upon the purse, and the four or five hundred pounds the farmer had saved out of the wreck of his affairs began to melt with terrible rapidity. When the Bath-chair was bought and the doctors were paid the two women sat down above the scanty accounts and looked at each other with foreboding faces.

' 'Zubah,' said the mother, beginning to cry and to embrace her daughter, 'what can we do? What *can* we do?' The girl offered no answer. 'We can just manage to live for a year, perhaps, and there's your father can never do a hand's turn again, and what can we do at the end of it? I'm afraid as you'll have to go out to service, my dear, though I never looked forrads to any of ours coming down so low as that. Miss Lording 'ud give you a place to be her maid, 'Zubah, and that 'ud be something off our shoulders.' Still the girl made no response. 'I'm afraid, 'Zubah, as your pride 'll never let you do that till you're forced to it.'

'My pride will not stand in my way, mother,' said Azubah, quietly, 'but I cannot help you and father by going into service. What are you to do when the year is over?'

'Perhaps Squire Carroll 'ud help us,' said the poor woman.

'Mother,' said the girl, ' haven't you heard father say over and over again that he wouldn't accept a favour at Mr. Carroll's hands? We must help ourselves.'

'And now,' said Mrs. Moore, 'my own child's a-turning contrairy.'

'No, no, dear,' answered her daughter, in a tone half-soothing and half-authoritative. 'We must be honourable, and we must support ourselves. I shall find something to do in less than a year which will keep us all.'

'Lord o' mercy!' cried the mother, 'what can *you* do to keep us all?'

'I have done something already, mother,' said Azubah. 'Not much, but something—a beginning. There is a paid choir at St. John's Church, and I saw an advertisement for a soprano—a treble, you know—and I answered it yesterday morning, and the curate heard me sing. He has the management of the choir, and he engaged me. It's not much, but twelve pounds a year is better than nothing at all, and it may lead to other things. There will be church concerts, and if I sing at them I am to have a guinea each time. I didn't tell you before, dear, because I wanted to surprise you.'

'My dear,' said the mother, 'you'll never ha' the courage to sing afore a churchful of folks.'

'Oh, yes,' answered Azubah, tranquilly. 'It was very unpleasant to have to sing to a stranger yesterday. But the more people there are to sing to, the easier it is. And, mother, another reason why I didn't tell you was that I wanted the first quarter's money to pay for singing lessons.'

'My dear, my dear!' cried the mother, 'we can't afford no such toying with Providence. We want to keep every penny we can get.'

'Mother,' said the girl, 'you remember young Mr. Carroll?'

'Surely.'

'You know how much he knew about music, and he always told me that if I liked to practise I should make a singer. I must try.'

'Your uncle Joshua had a lovely counter-tenor in his day,' said Mrs. Moore, who was a readily hopeful and easily desponding woman, 'an' your grandmother used to sing tribble in the old church at Overhill so as you could hear her all over the buildin'. The voice is a gift, and it runs in families. That's a thing as has been well understood always. A voice is a gift as runs in families.'

'Mother,' said the girl, anxiously, 'I feel so sure of being able to do something in that way for father and yourself, and there is so little time to be lost. I could go on improving all the time if you could let me have a little money to pay for lessons now instead of waiting a quarter of a year. I can pay you back again. There will be concerts at the church schools, and if I sing well they may lead to people asking me to sing at others. I will work hard, dear : I will indeed.'

The mother shook her head, but the denial was feeble, and her easily hopeful soul began to conjure up visions of her daughter as a great lady—almost like Jenny Lind, who was the one singer of note she had ever heard of.

'Here is an advertisement,' said the girl, passing a rapid finger over the columns of a newspaper ; 'the advertisement of an Italian lady, Signora—Signora—oh, here it is, Signora Malfi. Italians are always the best teachers, and Signora Malfi's terms are only five shillings for a lesson of an hour.'

'Lord o' mercy!' cried the good woman a second time, 'five shillings for an hour's squalling! Does she think folks are made o' money?'

But the daughter was the stronger, and the stronger won, as usual. Mr. Anthony Bethesda, who brought his Christian smile into the house with him before the settlement was half an hour old, was consulted on the question.

'I had not known it was so bad as this, dear friends,' said Mr. Bethesda; 'I would that I had known it earlier. There is a friend who keeps an office for registration in the City, and I would willingly have applied to him. There are temptations in the life upon which our sister proposes to embark.'

It was a pity, but Azubah could not be brought to endure Mr. Bethesda, and whilst he was talking she left the room. The girl was eager and enthusiastic, disposed to do everything she set about at once, and mightily scornful of the advice of people she did not like. Her heart was her judgment, and that, perhaps, was something of a pity also. Where she loved, she trusted the loved one's opinion —there had never been anybody quite so wise as her father—where she disliked, the wisdom of Solomon would have looked unwise. If Mr. Bethesda thought ill of her scheme the fact was almost a recommendation to it. It was at least an incentive to go on with it.

Azubah marched straight out of the house with the Signora Malfi's address in her purse, and very little else there. By dint of patient inquiry and one or two omnibus changes, she reached the Signora's residence, saw the lady, made terms, and actually took lesson Number

One at once. The Signora took the five shillings, and allowed her to carry away the bravura to study between lessons. It was then that Tom and Mark had seen her.

Whether the Italian young woman taught the English girl much that was of service to her is an open question, but the pupil worked devotedly, and made great progress. She was surprised at first to find that Mr. Bethesda had business at the West-end of London, but by-and-by she became used to seeing him, and even to accepting his casual escort home. There was not a doubt that Mr. Bethesda was a very good man, but it happens often in this topsy-turvy world that the naughty people are lovable, whilst the good are not, and somehow the girl and Mr. Bethesda made little progress towards friendship. Now, the Signora, who was not good, got on much better with Azubah, and began to take quite a motherly sort of interest in her, when, without warning of any sort, the musical student, calling at Signor Malfi's lodgings with intent to take the customary lesson, learned that the Signora had disappeared—had left England said the landlady.

Azubah being one of those young women who do things enthusiastically or not at all, had been full of day-dreams on her journey. But for those day-dreams it is pretty certain that she would never have struggled at all, for it was her truest nature to lie still to dream. They drew her on, however—pictures of full houses listening and murmurs of full-handed plaudits, years away as yet, and pictures of mother and father happily provided for and beyond the reach of care. The refusal at Signor Malfi's door quite froze the genial current of her soul, and the step which had been elastic in ascending went down the steps slow and leaden, and took her dispiritedly to the corner of the street.

'Miss Moore,' said a voice there, and Azubah looking up, saw the Signora. 'They told you I was gone away?' she asked.

'Yes,' said the girl in amazement.

'I have quarrelled,' said the Signora, 'with my husband. It will all be soon over, and I am not angry any more. He is angry yet. He is, like Italians, hot and jealous. I knew you would come, and I did not want you to be disappointed, and I had not your address. Therefore I came, and I am glad I saw you.'

Azubah was instantaneously certain that the Signora had been shamefully wronged. She was very glad to meet the swarthy lady, and shook hands with her warmly. What wretches men were, to be sure!

'I dare not let Tito see me now,' said the Signora. 'I am living half a mile away. If you will come to me I will give you your lessons.'

She would go certainly and help to defy

Tito and all his works. Five shillings a week was not much, but it was something, and she at least could be loyal to a woman in distress. The Signora was voluble in broken English on the way, and the girl's heart warmed at the recital of her wrongs.

'I will go upon the stage,' said Caterina in a while, 'and there I can keep myself. A lady can keep always herself upon the stage.'

They were in the new rooms by this time, in a house in the neighbourhood of Pimlico. The furniture, which had been extremely pretentious and gaudy, was dirty and dilapidated now. A white velvet hearthrug with broidered roses on it was turned up at the corners, and its flowers were frayed, and its whiteness was lost in innumerable stains of footsteps, ink, and wine. The mantel-shelf was clothed in ruby velvet, but the pile was mangy, and rubbed threadbare at the edges of the shelf as if by lounging shoulders. A man of the world would have known and read the signs of the place at a glance—but what was a girl of eighteen, country bred, to guess about them?

'But you cannot play in English,' said Azubah, in answer to Caterina's last speech.

'I shall sing,' said Caterina. She flung the piano open and began a vocal storm, shrieking through trills and melodies with amazing volume and shrillness. Azubah had never been at all inclined up to now to lay bare her hopes and desires to anybody, but there was that in the Signora's apparent helplessness and her loneliness, and most of all in her ambitions, which prompted the girl for the first time in her life to make a confidante. So when the shrieking melodies and trills were done with, she spoke and told her own story.

'You will sing well,' cried the Signora, 'when you have had more lessons. It is not harder for two than it is for one. We will learn duettos and sing them at the concerts together. You are white, and pale, and sorrowful, you little English flower,' she said, kissing Azubah, emphatically, 'and now it is plain the reason why. And you are good, and that is why I like you.'

A week earlier the girl would have resented Caterina's caresses almost as much as those of a man, but now the Signora was in trouble and Azubah's heart warmed to her. Besides, this promise seemed to open up a way to her ambitions. The whole afternoon was spent in practice, and when the five shillings came to be paid, the Italian woman took them lingeringly as though she would fain refuse them.

When Azubah paid her next visit a little fat man with a bald head, ruddy lips, and beady eyes sat in the Signora's sitting-room listening to her as she sang.

'This is my lady friend,' said the Signora, bouncing from the piano when her song was

done, and embracing Azubah vehemently.
'This, my child, is Mistare Moss; he is of the
—how do you say, Mistare Moss?'

'The Megatherium,' said Mr. Moss, turning
the m's into b's.

'It is very good place to sing at,' said
Caterina, 'is it not, Mistare Moss?'

'It is one of the best in London,' said Mr.
Moss, nosily. 'It's not so long established as
some of 'em, but what we want there is genuine
talent. We're open to give genuine talent a
start in almost any direction.'

'Let my lady friend sing,' said the Signora,
'then we will sing a duetto together.' She
turned to Azubah, 'Let Mr. Moss hear you.'

Azubah took off her gloves and sat down at
the piano with a beating heart. What did
she know? The Megatherium Concert Hall
was quite outside her experiences, and the
gentleman said it was one of the best places to
sing at in London. Through him might lie

the avenue to fortune. Her fingers touched the keys firmly and lightly. The piano had seen its best days certainly, but it was fairly in tune, and its voice gave her new confidence. She began to sing 'As pants the hart for cooling streams when heated in the chase.' The Signora listened doubtfully and glanced at Mr. Moss.

'Very dice, biss,' said Mr. Moss. 'Very dice iddeed, but not the Begatheriub style. We don't go id for religious busic there. Try agaid. Subthig lighter if you please—subthig operatic.'

Azubah's more familiar music was mostly antiquated, and after the Signora she was afraid to try the something operatic. Her own mellow and liquid-sounding tones fell on the ear with double sweetness after the shrill notes of Caterina's voice, but she did not guess that, and was afraid of being overmatched. So she chose Barnett's old-fashioned 'Rise, gentle

Moon,' and sang it so well that Mr. Moss applauded softly.

'Yes, biss,' he said, 'that will do. Try agaid. A ballad is the sort of thing to suit you, I fadcy. Try a ballad.' She tried a ballad. 'Not quite the stage style,' said Mr. Moss. 'A little broader and then you'll do. A leetle broader. Well, ladies, I shall have no objection to give you an opportunity. You can have a week begiddig on Bonday dext, two turns a-piece. Thed, if you suit us, we can talk about terms afterwards. The opening,' he continued, 'is valuable, of course, but we don't ask for anything in the way of premiub. We give you a chadce od your berits.'

Whether Mr. Moss were a gentleman or not Azubah could not tell. He was not in the least like Squire Carroll, or his son Tom, or the Vicar, or the Curate at Overhill, or Mr. Lording, the father of her old patroness and friend. He wore a prodigious deal of jewellery and he was not particularly clean about the hands; but little as the girl knew, she had heard that artists were often untidy. Mr. Moss no doubt mixed much with artists even if he himself were not of the brotherhood, and perhaps he had caught their manners and customs. And how fortunate she herself was to have found such a chance so soon! If she succeeded—oh, if she *only* could succeed! Father and mother need never want for anything. Her fortune was made and theirs along with it. The Signora was confident of taking the world by storm now that she had at last secured an opportunity for making her voice heard. Opera managers all over Europe had been blind to the treasure they had thrown away. Whatever faults Tito had, he could sing and he knew what singing should be. Tito had always been indignant at the blindness of the managers.

Arrangements were completed with business-like brevity, and Azubah found herself pledged to sing nightly for a week before an audience of whom she knew nothing. The Signora had earned the right to kiss her and to be friendly with her, having secured her this unexampled piece of good fortune. But the girl's head was turning and her heart was beating with it all as she went home that evening.

'You oughtn't to be going out at night alone, my dear,' said her mother anxiously, when she heard the news. 'And yet your father isn't in a case to be left for an hour.'

'Signora Malfi is going as well,' said Azubah. 'I shall be quite safe with her.'

'Signora Malfi,' sounded grandly on the unsophisticated country woman's ears, and Mrs. Moore knew already that Signor Malfi was or had been a singer at Her Majesty's Opera, and naturally set him down as being somehow on the Royal staff, and more or less intimately associated with the Queen herself. So that the association of her daughter with these high personages was altogether a thing to be thankful for. Not that she thought much of foreigners as a rule, but Her Majesty's foreigners were necessarily superior to the crowd.

The girl had little difficulty with her mother, who was more proud than anxious, but she had many tremors in her own behalf. The wished-for, dreaded night came at last, and she hastened to the Signora's rooms, there to dress by appointment. Caterina, with bare arms and shoulders glittering with powder, stood aghast at the plainness of her protégé's attire; but it was too late to change it, even if Azubah had had the wardrobe of a princess— which she had not.

The Signora, with all her finery carefully shawled, led the way and called a four-wheeler, and the two were driven to the Megatherium stage-door. Mr. Moss's duties happening to have called him there at that moment, he received them.

'Good eveding, ladies. Glad to see you. You can have a dressing-roob betweed you to-borrow. I'll see to it. Come this way.'

It was all unaccustomed and strange to Azubah, who began to feel curiously nervous and elevated by turns. The dust, the dirt, the bare unplastered walls, the slips of scenery, lines of rope, coils of gas tubing, the olla podrida of stage. odds and ends made an un-pleasant impression upon her. She had never so much as read a description of the view behind the scenes, and had expected something like a vestry at church or a school committee-room to wait in. There was the sound of a big band from the front, and in the frowsy green-room a man and a woman in grotesque attire and painted faces awaited their call. In a minute the tones of the band softened down and a raucous voice began to sing. The voice and the tune were things to shudder at, but the words were indistinguishable. After frequent repetition of the air the voice ceased, a great noise of applause was heard, and a young man put in his head at the doorway and nodded familiarly at the grotesquely-dressed couple. This young man was in evening dress, and his lower man looked passable, but he wore a fiery-red wig and his face was painted in exaggerated semblance of a drunkard's.

'See you at Bobbos's, shan't I?' he asked. 'I've sent the orfice to Bill and Judy. Ta-tar.'

Altogether, except for the near neighbourhood of the band, it was extremely unlike an evening concert, and Azubah was puzzled and dispirited.

'The Deutchers!' cried a small boy, thrusting his ragged head under the young man's arm. The grotesquely-dressed people passed out and the band began again. The Deutchers appeared to score a great success, for they returned twice to the stage, amid resounding plaudits. Again Azubah heard the voices, and was inclined to think but little of the vocal powers of the singers at the Megatherium. Was it at all the place Mr. Moss had represented it as being?

'Snorer Cateriner!' cried the ragged-headed boy when the Deutchers had completed their third ditty. The Signora arose and slipped her shawl from her gleaming shoulders. As she passed through the doorway another figure or two appeared—one lady in tights and a remarkably short dress, and another in appropriate concert costume. Azubah listened for her friend's voice and heard it shriller and higher and louder than ever, ringing through the place to the accompaniment of a piano. There was a noise of applause at the close of her song, and she swept radiant to the door of the green-room, nodded, and swept back again. She sang a second time, and the applause was louder than before. Then, after a long interval, during which the band played the same air over and over again monotonously, to the sole accompaniment so far as Azubah's ears could tell her of an irregular thumping upon the platform, the ragged-headed boy made another appearance.

'Mam'selle Mora,' said the boy.

'Go,' said Caterina, pushing her gently. 'That is you. Here is your first song. Why do you shake so? Go. I will go with you.'

There were other people in the room again, and the Signora spoke in a whisper. Azubah obeyed her, and almost before she knew it found herself upon a stage with a row of footlights in front which, for the first moment or two, obscured the hall beyond. She heard a piano playing the overture to 'Rise, gentle Moon,' and in due time she began to sing. At the end of the first verse a man rapped vigorously with a hammer upon a table, and there was a faint scattered sound of applause about the hall. Then her sight came to her, and she saw a crowded auditorium, in which men sat smoking and drinking. It was not what she had looked to find, and she felt debased and degraded, but at least she would not break down before all these people. She took up the air at the due time, and sang again as she had never dared to sing before. The place seemed so vast to her that she dared, for the first time in her life, to give her voice full scope. She disdained the people, and she hated herself for being there. She would not strain her power by a thread's breadth to please them, but the freedom of the long and lofty hall invited her, and, half to her own amazement, her voice filled it with sound. The applause at the end of the second verse was considerable, and in spite of her disdain and disappointment at the place and people, she was conscious of a sense of elation as she walked from the stage with no answering salute. It was by pure accident that she went off on the right side, and met the Signora in the flies.

'Mademoiselle Mora will appear again,' said a loud voice, and the tapping on the table began again.

'Your music,' whispered the Signora, thrusting one roll into her hand and taking away the other. 'Go. They are ready for you.'

She walked proudly back with the music clenched tightly in her gloved hand. She had been tricked into coming here, though she scarcely knew whom to blame; yet, being here, she would not fail. The pianist began 'The Banks of Allan Water,' and she sang the first verse with conscious power. But as she opened her lips for the second she saw directly beneath and before her a face familiar from childhood, and this so froze her that the musician had to try back again. The face she had seen was Mark Carroll's, and her eyes roving helplessly from his recognising gaze encountered another glance—Tom Carroll's this time. It would have been bitter enough to have been seen there by anybody who knew her when Michael Moore had held his head high in the world, but to be met there by him, and to be hopeless of telling him by what an error she came there, seemed for the moment a thing too shameful to be borne. The pianist was nearing the note once more, and she nerved herself to the task and struggled through the song. She knew that she was singing badly, that she was out of time and tune, and she was prepared for the ominous silence which met her at the close.

'You'll do better to-morrow,' said Mr. Moss, kindly enough, as she quitted the stage.

'I think it right to tell you, sir,' she answered quietly, 'that I shall not be here to-morrow. Signora Malfi,' flashing round upon her with widening eyes and clenched hands, 'how dared you bring me to a place like this?'

'Moore was a very proud fellow,' Tom was saying to his cousin. 'He would never have allowed the girl to appear in a place like this unless something had happened to him. I must hunt him up.'

'Oh,' said Mark, carelessly, 'I suppose the Signora brought her here. She doesn't sing badly. It's a bit of an adventure, though, to find two lady acquaintances on the Megatherium stage in one evening. Malfi has kicked the charming Caterina out, I suppose,' he added to himself. 'That is my fault, and does me an honour of which I am hardly worthy. It's a very appropriate line of life for her, and she'll do well at it. These dunderheads fancy she can sing. The little girl's worth fifty of her. Mark, I think you must look up the playmate of your childhood. She's growing absolutely pretty.'

CHAPTER XII.

WHEN Mark turned after these reflections his cousin Tom had disappeared.

'He'll be back to see Léonie,' said Mark, and thought no more about it. Mademoiselle Léonie (otherwise Mrs. Whitehouse) was attracting all London, more or less, by her mid-air somersault in full flight from one trapeze bar to another, and Tom and Mark were there to see her. The performance came on, and in due time was over, and Tom had not returned. In point of fact, Tom had found other business. He was always a bit of a Quixote, and the sight of his old playfellow on a music-hall stage seemed to speak so plainly of some sort of misfortune that he went out at once to find out what the misfortune was, and, if it might be, to alleviate it.

'You can't go in, sir,' said the keeper of the stage-door, with inflexible aspect.

'Take in my card to Miss Moore,' said Tom, and at a half-crown presented with the card the door-keeper grew suddenly flexible, and obeyed. Tom followed in his footsteps, and by-and-by came upon a scene of quarrel, in which the persons concerned were the Signora and Mr. Moss.

'You cad say what you like,' cried Mr. Moss, 'it's all the sabe to me. It's the pridciple of the thig I go for. The yug woman's billed for a week, ad she'll have to appear for a week. She aid't ady particular catch neither, but I'm goig to stick to the bargain.'

Azubah, with an extremely white face, was trying to get past Mr. Moss, and Mr. Moss by much adroit dodging frustrated her at every move.

'Allow the lady to pass, if you please,' said Tom, in a tone a shade too decided to sound civil to a stranger. Mr. Moss regarded him angrily, and demanded to know who he was and how he came there. These inquiries were presented with more than necessary emphasis, and accompanied by some grossnesses of expression which were part of Mr. Moss's common conversational stock-in-trade. They sounded horrible to the gentleman, used as they were in the presence of women. 'Stand aside,' cried Tom. 'Allow me, Miss Moore.' His command to Mr. Moss was enforced by a strong but quiet hand; the girl took the protecting arm and clung to it, and she and Tom moved together towards the stairs which led to the street-door. The manager in a fury declared that the intruder should repent this, and roared for a policeman. Then running forward, he stood half-way down the stairs to intercept Tom's exit, and a most unfortunate thing happened. Mr. Moss standing there bellowing blasphemy and blocking the way so incensed Tom Carroll that he took him by the collar and swung him down such of the stairs as still remained to be traversed.

At this Tom was seized from behind, and a dreadful hubbub arose, Mr. Moss holding his nose and cursing through it, the Signora shrieking from the top of the stairs, and the whole available talent of the Megatherium Concert Hall swelling the chorus which accompanied this duet. In the middle of it all somebody brought a policeman, and the noise redoubled, and somehow, when Tom had tendered his card, they all surged out together into the street, Azubah still clinging to her too-impetuous protector's arm, frightened and white, but for all that self-possessed and silent.

The card was not enough. It was evident, said the policeman, that a serious assault had been committed, and the gentleman must come to the station. On his own authority the policeman could not let the gentleman go.

Things began to look exceedingly unpleasant for Tom, but having got himself into the position, he bore it as well as he could, demanded a cab, which was brought with difficulty through the crowd, saw Azubah into it, paid the cabman his fare beforehand, and then finding another hansom for himself and the policeman, submitted to be driven to the station, leaving Mr. Moss to follow. The district police-office being very near at hand, he had the satisfaction of being followed by a score or two of the onlookers.

Mr. Moss appeared with his nose bleeding, and his charge against Tom was that he had forced his way through the stage-door, and had there, without provocation, grievously assaulted him—Mr. Moss. To this Tom answered coldly and contemptuously with a statement of the facts, and again proffered his card. The inspector regretted that he could not accept that as a sufficient guarantee of the gentleman's identity, and offered an alternative suggestion. Mr. Carroll might either go home, accompanied by a policeman, who would be instructed to ascertain the accuracy or non-accuracy of his professed address, or he might send for a friend who would become surety for his appearance on the morrow.

All this was more and more unpleasant to a sensitive youngster who had gone out to relieve distress and had met with so poor a reward for good intentions, and Tom was naturally indignant at it. But he made shift to control himself and to write a brief note to his cousin Mark, whom he described so particularly to the officer that that functionary had no difficulty in finding him at the place at which Tom had left him. He glanced at the note and rose tranquilly.

'What is the matter?' he asked, on reaching

the street. The official told the story as he knew it. 'Nonsense,' said Mark decisively. 'Mr. Carroll is one of the best tempered and gentlest fellows in the world. He must have received great provocation.'

Mr. Mark Carroll, of Pump Court, Temple, barrister-at-law, having identified his cousin, and having become surety for his appearance, Tom was released, and went on his way much perturbed. Mark accompanied him home, and they talked the matter over on the way.

'You'll get a solicitor to instruct me, as a matter of form,' said Mark, 'and I'll defend the case. All these fellows are servants of Mr. Moss, and they'll lie of course till they're black in the face. Your only witnesses are the two women. I shall have a chance of airing my Italian with the Signora.'

He laughed at that fancy. It was certainly an odd chance which would throw them together in a police-court as barrister and witness. Tom broke in on the current of his thoughts.

'You don't suppose, Mark, that I am going to drag that poor little girl's name into an affair like this?'

'Good gracious!' cried Mark. 'Why not? She is your principal witness. Moss's men will all swear what Moss wants them to swear—that's human nature. The poor devils have to live one way or another, and a little perjury is all in the day's work when it's wanted. Your case is this. Being a person of known bene-volence'—there Mark smiled his own pleasant smile—'and observing on the stage of the Megatherium a young lady whose parents were once prosperous tenants on your father's estate (a very good point that father's estate), you arrive at the natural conclusion that her parents are either lost or have fallen into finan-cial difficulties. With that warm-hearted im-pulsiveness which is known to be your chief characteristic, you go round to the back of the stage to see if you can be of service. You find the young lady being horribly bullied by the manager, why and wherefore we at present know not, and you interfere mildly for her protection. You admit that for the lady's protection you laid your hand upon Mr. Moss. Mr. Moss unfortunately fell downstairs.'

'No,' said Tom; 'I threw him downstairs, and he deserved it. If I had broken his neck I should have had no pity for him.'

'That would have been manslaughter,' said Mark, smilingly. 'And, of course, you threw him downstairs, and no doubt he deserved it. But it is the rule to admit nothing in these cases.'

'I shall tell the truth,' said Tom hotly. 'I'll have none of your confounded legal lies.'

'Tell the truth and shame the devil, eh? Well, that's a proverb, and there's some of the wisdom of our ancestors in it no doubt. "Tell the truth and go to the devil" would do for a revised edition. Leave the case to me, Tom. My conscience is a little tougher than your own.'

'You want to drag Miss Moore's name into it?' asked Tom, who was not by any means in his usual state of placid good temper.

'My dear fellow,' cried Mark, 'you can't do without it.'

'But I *can* do without it,' cried Tom, in great heat, 'and I *will* do without it. What does it matter to me? People whose opinion I value know that I am no brawler, and the people whose opinion I don't value can think what they please.'

'My dear fellow,' began Mark again, but Tom stopped him.

'I won't hear any more about it, Mark. I shall go down to-morrow, and what happens will happen. But I will have no lies told or suggested in my behalf, and I won't have the name of poor Moore's daughter dragged into the affair at all.'

'You seem tender about poor Moore's daughter,' said Mark, with an open sneer. He thought he had never heard of anything so downright foolish as the view Tom took of this business.

'I am tender about Moore's daughter,' answered Tom, coldly. 'I hope I should be tender about the daughter of any old friend in such a matter.'

'Well, now,' said Mark, 'if Miss Moore is to be left out what brought you there at all? It's a case of wanton and purposeless intrusion at once.'

Tom, seeing how untenable his position was against any reasonable assault, naturally held to it all the more doggedly.

'Well, Tom,' said his cousin, 'you know how much I like you, but I'm bound to tell you that in this case you are acting like an ass.'

'And you,' Tom answered, 'advise me to act like a cad and a coward.'

Mark shrugged his shoulders, and was silent. It was evident that Tom was not in a mood to be reasoned with, and if in this case he chose to act like a fool, one man, at least, had done his duty and had warned him. Mark had no inclination to be a martyr in the case, as he would be if he offended Tom too far by his interference. Tom was too valuable a friend to be offended lightly, and if he would not be helped out of this awkward scrape he must get out of it by himself as best he could. So the two cousins parted for the night somewhat coolly.

On the morrow they met at the police-office, where, by Mark's interference, one discomfort was spared to the most prominent criminal of the day, and Tom was allowed to take a seat at the table in place of appearing in the dock. Mark had done more than this before-hand. He had met the presiding magistrate once or twice, and had taken advantage of that fact to call upon him early in the morning and to relate his cousin's case.

'My cousin, sir,' said Mark, ' is the most Quixotic fool alive. There is a most perfect defence to the case, and he will not use it. He has no earthly reason to consider the girl, except that she is the daughter of an old tenant of his father's.'

'I must go by the evidence, Mr. Carroll,' said the magistrate. 'I can't allow myself to be affected by an ex parte statement.'

'God forbid!' cried Mark, piously. 'My only object in calling upon you was to explain the case for my cousin's benefit with you personally, and not in your capacity as magistrate. You are an old acquaintance of his father's, and if any questions are asked and you are able to say on my authority that a complete defence existed, but was not brought forward from motives of exaggerated delicacy——'

'I can refer the inquirers to Mr. Mark

Carroll,' said the magistrate; and there the conversation ended.

It came to pass, in consequence of Mark's manœuvre, that the magistrate handled Tom gently, and the result was that the misdemeanant was fined ten pounds, which was paid at once, and as a matter of course. And if the affair could have ended there it would have passed off lightly enough. But everybody knows what a hungry interest attaches to matters theatrical in the public mind, and the Megatherium, though not exactly a theatre, was next door to it. The one reporter who sat in this particular court, and was paid twopence a line by the daily papers, not for what he wrote, but for what they published, hailed the case as a God-send, and took a keen verbatim note, manifolded it in long-hand, and sent it to every journal in the metropolis. The bills of the evening papers made a special line of the case, and the morning papers headed it,

'Unprovoked Assault.' The *Mirror* had an indignant article on the shameless indulgence displayed by the magistrate towards the ruffianly defendant, who, without being able to plead even the ordinary excuse of drunkenness, had forced his way into a scene of peaceful business, and without rhyme or reason assaulted the manager of the Megatherium in the execution of his duty.

The *Mirror*, being a Tory journal of the highest and dryest sort, was naturally on Mr. Carroll's breakfast-table every morning. In its columns Mr. Carroll read the dreadful story, and whilst he sat in a condition of horrified amazement, Lording, who was an earlier riser and had seen the news at breakfast an hour before, came bursting in impetuously.

'This is all some horrible mistake,' he said, seeing at a glance that Mr. Carroll had read the news. 'Some scoundrel has taken a respectable name. I want you to wire to Tom and demand the truth about the matter.'

'I shall go up to town immediately,' said Mr. Carroll, ruffling with injured majesty. It would have been bad enough for any father to read such a record of a son, but he suffered in proportion to his pride, and that being abnormal, so were his pains.

'I will come with you,' answered Lording. 'Mary knows nothing about the matter, and I have burned the daily papers. If you'll let me write a note here and send one of your men over with it, he can take my horse and leave him.'

'Certainly,' said Mr. Carroll. He bore the misery of the news firmly and like a man.

Lording wrote a brief note to his daughter, saying that important business called him up to London, and asking that a portmanteau might be sent on to him. He added that Mr. Carroll accompanied him, and that put it into the girl's head at once that something had happened to Tom. She sent a note by the groom who drove back her father's messenger, demanding to know if anything were the matter. Lording, thinking the deceit justifiable, scrawled a hasty line to say that there was nothing on earth to be alarmed at ; and he had, indeed, quite persuaded himself that somebody had been impersonating Tom Carroll. There was nothing easier than to offer a card that belonged to somebody else in an affair of that sort, and Tom had always been so much a gentleman that it was impossible to think of him as being thus suddenly transformed into a rowdy.

The two elders had no heart for talk as they travelled to London, and a more and more unpleasant dread lest the thing should prove true after all began to settle down on both of them.

'I'll tell you what, Carroll,' said Lording, at Euston, ' I won't interfere with your talk with the lad. It will be better for you and him to have it out together. I'll go and see Mark. The two are always together, and he's bound to know something about it. If he doesn't I shall follow you to Tom's place, for I can't stand the suspense and I must know the truth.'

'As you will,' said Mr. Carroll frozenly, and they parted on their separate ways.

Lording found Mark at home.

'What's all this in the papers about Tom?' he cried. 'Do *you* know anything about it? Is it true?'

'Well,' Mark answered, 'it is and it isn't.'

'Hang it all, man!' cried Lording, 'don't offer me riddles. What is it? Tell me what you know.'

'Well,' said Mark, 'there's a lady in the case, and Tom has some high-flown notions about its being dishonourable to put her in the witness-box to clear him.'

'A lady in the case?' said Lording, blankly. 'Confound him! And confound you, too! Can't you tell a plain tale, and be hanged to you?'

Thus adjured, Mark told the story as he knew it, and Lording breathed freely.

'It's abominably unpleasant, and all that, of course,' said the good old boy. 'But we who know the lad can trust him, eh, Mark? He's in the right, is Tom, quite in the right. And what on earth can be the matter with poor Moore to let his girl get into a place like that? My daughter's quite savage at the girl not writing to her. She's sent three letters and not had a line in answer. I say Mark, there must have been a good deal of hard swearing against Tom. Eh?'

'About half a dozen of the witnesses went for flat perjury, according to Tom's story,' answered Mark. 'I told him what an ass he was not to have a defence. I could have made those fellows contradict each other a thousand times over. But Tom's a Quixote.'

'I like him the better for it,' said Lording. 'As honest-hearted and truthful a lad as breathes. A fine, high-minded, honourable lad, by gad, sir ! And all the same, its abominably unpleasant to have these things said of one and not to be able to deny them.'

Nothing that happened to other people affected Mark greatly, as a rule, but for once a circumstance outside his own interests almost cost him his temper.

'I'm glad for Tom's sake that you approve of him,' he said. 'Personally—if my opinion's of any value—I think him the most unmitigated ass in Europe. Look at the pain he gives you,' cried Mark, not because he cared for that, but to make good his argument. 'Look at the pain he gives his father ! And all for a girl for whom he has no business to care a farthing.'

'I suppose,' said Lording, 'he cares no more for her than he has a right to care for her.'

'That's his concern,' said Mark, ill-temperedly. 'You had better ask him.' Lording was not a thin-skinned man, and Mark knew when brusquerie of manner was harmless to himself, and when it was likely to be harmful. To the people from whom he expected nothing, he could afford to be impolite if it suited him. He was a little sore about this matter of Tom's also, because he had calculated on being employed for the defence, and might very easily have borrowed a fifty on the strength of it, for of course he could not dream of accepting a fee from his cousin for such a service.

Lording looked serious for a moment, but whatever fancy assailed him, he dismissed it.

'Your uncle is in town,' he said, 'and has gone to see Tom. Perhaps we had better walk up and help to smooth things.'

Mark acceded, and the two drove to Montague Gardens together. There they found father and son at decided loggerheads, the elder in a cold rage, and the younger in a hot one.

'I have never given you the right to doubt my word,' Tom was saying loudly as they entered, 'I never told you a lie in my life, and I claim your credence for my version of the story as a right.'

'And I demand that if your tale be true, sir,' his father answered him, 'you prosecute those low fellows for perjury, and clear your name of the stain which rests upon it.' The old man was naturally indignant. There is pretty generally some right on both sides in a real quarrel between people who have cared for each other. 'It is an insult personal to myself,' said Mr. Carroll, swelling himself anew now that he had an audience, 'that such an imputation should rest upon my son.' Tom was very near yielding. After all, was Miss Moore's privacy in a matter like this to be set against his father's peace of mind? He had not thought about this side of the question until now, and it moved him a good deal. But Mr. Carroll could not let well alone, and unfortunately he went on, 'Whom am I to believe, the six or seven sworn witnesses in the case who appeared, sir, in the light of day, or the person who was incriminated by their evidence, and who declines to take steps for the clearance of his character? Declines,' said Mr. Carroll, with a white face turned towards his only son, 'on a pretence so flimsy and absurd that I can but look upon it as a subterfuge.'

'Am I to understand,' asked Tom, with a rather wicked-sounding repression in his voice, 'that you refuse to accept my word upon this matter?'

'Unless you substantiate it, certainly,' said Mr. Carroll, loftily. 'The story as you relate it is sufficiently dishonouring to me, but until you establish it I must prefer to believe the other and the worse.'

'That is very unfortunate for both of us,' said Tom, quietly. After that wild horses would not have drawn him to an exculpation of himself.

'Tom,' cried Lording, 'you mustn't leave your father in this way. Carroll, be reasonable.'

The youngster had gathered up hat and stick and gloves, and was making for the door.

'My dear uncle,' cried Mark, 'forgive me if I suggest that you are both a little heated at this moment. I am sure Tom's story is the true one.'

If Tom and his father quarrelled, half Mark's income stood in peril.

'What do you know about the matter, Mark?' inquired Mr. Carroll.

'I have Tom's word,' said Mark. His uncle turned away with a mere wave of the hand, and as he turned he faced Tom, who felt his father's gesture almost unbearably insulting.

'My father cannot accept my word,' he said, controlling himself to outer quiet. 'That is very unhappy for us both, but my fault by no means.'

'You shan't go,' cried Lording with an oath, stepping in between Tom and the door.

'*I* will go,' said Mr. Carroll, taking up his hat. 'Nephew Mark—may I ask that you will give me your arm? Shall I see you before you leave town, Lording? Good-day, sir,' turning to his son, 'and good-bye.'

'You shan't go either,' cried Lording again, setting his back against the door.

'Sir!' said Mr. Carroll, with pompous passion, 'stand aside. I can manage my family affairs without extraneous assistance. I disown that fellow. He is no son of mine any longer. I repudiate all claims he may make upon me.'

'Go your way,' said Lording, puffing and blowing with rage at the other's tone towards him, 'you pompous idiot, go your way. But mark my words, you'll be sorry for this to the day of your death.'

Mr. Carroll, with his white face suddenly grown scarlet, stood waiting for Mark's arm. Mark, with an apologetic glance at Tom and Lording, offered it, and the two marched out of the room and down the stairs together. The two who were left behind stood agaze at each other, listening to the creak of Carroll's footsteps on the stairs, to the jar of bolt and chain as the door opened, and the crash with which it closed behind him.

END OF THE FIRST VOLUME.

LONDON : PRINTED BY
SPOTTISWOODE AND CO., NEW-STREET SQUARE
AND PARLIAMENT STREET

www.ingramcontent.com/pod-product-compliance
Lightning Source LLC
Chambersburg PA
CBHW060515030726
47498CB00004B/954